Louise couldn't qu... On almost every ... were candles, and ... brightly. There was holly and ivy on the mantel, and in the corner, near one of the windows...a Christmas tree!

Not a huge one, but at least five feet high, bare except for a silver star on top. She spotted a box of decorations sitting on the floor, waiting to be hung. She picked a bauble out of the box and fingered it gently.

How…? Who…? Ben!

Not knowing what else to do, she sat cross-legged in front of the fire, staring at the patterns on the tiles until they danced in front of her eyes. Was this guy for real? Tears sprang to her eyes and she wiped them away hastily. No one had ever gone out of their way to do something so special for her before.

Louise stood up and placed a hand over her mouth. Oh, this was dangerous. All at once she saw the folly of her whole "daydreaming is safe" plan. It was backfiring spectacularly. Her mind now constantly drifted toward Ben Oliver. And now her brain was starting to clamor for more than just fantasies. Especially when he did things like this. She was aching for all the *moments* she'd rehearsed in her head to become real.…

Dear Reader,

Everyone has their own family Christmas traditions, don't they? I discovered that all-important fact when I got married. In my family we used to rush downstairs on Christmas morning and tear open our presents before breakfast. Imagine the sheer self-restraint I had to show when I discovered that my husband's family opened theirs *after* Christmas dinner, and only when all the washing up was done and everyone had a cup of tea in their hands. How I managed to hold out that first year, I'll never know.

Anyway, my husband and I have managed to combine our families' different Christmas cultures and have come up with a few of our own, too. One thing I absolutely cannot be without on Christmas day is bread sauce! It sounds odd, but it's a traditional English accompaniment to roast turkey, and so easy to make!

First, fill a pan with a pint of milk. Stud an onion with three cloves and place in the milk, along with a bay leaf. Bring the milk to a boil, then remove from the heat. Discard the onion and the bay leaf, add four ounces of white breadcrumbs and season. Cook for five minutes, stirring until the sauce has thickened. Remove from the heat and stir in one ounce of butter and four tablespoons of single cream. Spoon into a serving dish, sprinkle with grated nutmeg and, *voilà,* you have a little bit of heaven to go with your Christmas lunch. Once you've tried it, you'll never go back—I promise!

Christmas blessings and a happy New Year.

Fiona Harper

FIONA HARPER

Christmas Wishes,
Mistletoe Kisses

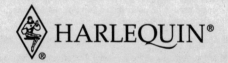

HARLEQUIN®

TORONTO • NEW YORK • LONDON
AMSTERDAM • PARIS • SYDNEY • HAMBURG
STOCKHOLM • ATHENS • TOKYO • MILAN • MADRID
PRAGUE • WARSAW • BUDAPEST • AUCKLAND

ISBN-13: 978-0-373-17552-9
ISBN-10:   0-373-17552-3

CHRISTMAS WISHES, MISTLETOE KISSES

First North American Publication 2008.

www.eHarlequin.com

Printed in U.S.A.

As a child, **Fiona Harper** was constantly teased for either having her nose in a book or living in a dream world. Things haven't changed much since then, but at least in writing she's found a use for her runaway imagination. After studying dance at university, Fiona worked as a dancer, teacher and choreographer, before trading in that career for video editing and production. When she became a mother she cut back on her working hours to spend time with her children, and when her littlest one started preschool she found a few spare moments to rediscover an old but not forgotten love—writing.

Fiona lives in London, but her other favorite places to be are the Highlands of Scotland and the Kent countryside on a summer's afternoon. She loves cooking good food and anything cinnamon-flavored. Of course she still can't keep away from a good book, or a good movie—especially romances—but only if she's stocked up with tissues, because she knows she will need them by the end, be it happy or sad. Her favorite things in the world are her wonderful husband, who has learned to decipher her incoherent ramblings, and her two daughters.

For Mum, I love you.

CHAPTER ONE

MOST women would have given at least one kidney to be in Louise's shoes—both literally and figuratively. The shoes in question were hot off the Paris catwalk, impossibly high heels held to her foot by delicately interwoven silver straps. The main attraction, however, was the man sitting across the dinner table from her. The very same hunk of gorgeousness who had topped a magazine poll of 'Hollywood's Hottest' only last Thursday.

Louise stared at her cutlery, intent on tracing a figure of eight pattern on her dessert spoon and eavesdropped on conversations in the busy restaurant. Other people's conversations. Other people's lives.

Her dinner companion shifted in his seat and the heel of his boot made jarring contact with the little toe of her right foot. She jerked away and leaned over to rub it.

'Thanks a bunch, Toby!' she said, glaring at him from half under the table.

Toby stopped grinning at a pair of bleached blonde socialites who were in the process of wafting past their table and turned to face her, eyebrows raised. 'What?'

'Never mind,' she muttered and sat up straight again, carefully crossing her ankles and tucking them under her chair. Her little toe was still warm and pulsing.

The waiter appeared with their exquisite-looking entrées and

Toby's eyebrows relaxed back into their normal 'sexily brooding' position as he started tearing into his guinea-fowl. Louise's knife and fork stayed on the tablecloth.

He hadn't even bothered with his normal comments about the carbs on her plate. She was supposed to be getting rid of that baby weight, remember? Never mind that Jack had just turned eight. His father was still living in a dream world if he thought she was going to be able to squeeze back into those size zero designer frocks hanging in the back of her wardrobe.

But then Toby had emotionally checked out of their marriage some time ago. She kept up the pretence for Jack's sake, posed and smiled for the press and celebrity magazines and fiercely denied any rumours of a rift. He hadn't ever said he'd stopped loving her, but it was evident in the things he *didn't* do, the things he *didn't* say. And then there was the latest rumour...

She picked up her cutlery and attacked her pasta.

'Slow down, Lulu! No one's timing you,' Toby said, eyes still on his plate.

Lulu. When they'd first met, she'd thought it had been cute that he'd picked up on, and used, her baby brother's attempts at her name. Lulu was exotic, exciting...and a heck of a lot more inter-esting than plain old Louise. She'd liked being Lulu back then.

Now she just wanted him to see *Louise* again. She stopped eating and looked at him, waiting for him to raise his head, give her a smile, his trademark cheeky wink—anything.

He waved for the waiter and asked for another bottle of wine. Then she saw him glance across and nod at the two blondes, now seated a few tables away, but not once in the next ten minutes did he look at her. Her seat might as well have been empty.

'Toby?'

'What?' Finally he glanced in her direction. But once, where she had been able to see her dreams coming to life, there was only a vacancy.

He rubbed his front tooth with his forefinger and it made a

horrible squeaking noise. 'Do I have spinach on my teeth, or something?'

She shook her head. What spinach would dare sully the picture of masculine perfection sitting opposite her? The thought was almost sacrilegious. She was tempted to laugh.

The words wouldn't come. How did you ask what she wanted to ask? And how did you stand the answer?

She tried to say it with her eyes instead. When she'd been modelling, photographers had always raved about the 'intensity' in her eyes. She tried to show it all—the emptiness inside her, the magnetic force that kept the pair of them revolving around each other, the small spark of hope that hadn't quite been extinguished yet. If he'd just do it once…really connect with her…

'Jeez, Lulu. Cheer up, will—'

A chime from the phone in his pocket interrupted him. He slid it out and held it shielded in his hand and slightly under the table. The only change in his features was a slight curve of his bottom lip. *Now* he looked at her properly. He searched her face for a reaction, and then returned the mobile to his jacket pocket and returned his gaze to his plate.

She waited.

He shrugged. 'Work stuff. You know…'

Unfortunately she had the feeling that she did know. And she kept knowing all the way through dinner as she shoved one forkful after another into her mouth, tasting nothing.

The rumour was true.

All afternoon, since she'd spoken to her friend on the phone, she'd hoped it was all silly speculation, someone putting two and two together and coming up with five. Six years ago, when the tabloids had been jumping with the stories of Toby's 'secret love trysts' with his leading lady, she'd refused to believe it, had given interview after interview denying there had been any truth in it. During the second 'incident' she'd done the same but, while her outward performance had been just as impassioned, inside she'd been counting all the things that hadn't added up: the hushed phone calls, the extra meetings with his agent. Never enough to pin him down, but just enough to make her die a little more each time she shook her head for the reporters and dismissed it as nonsense.

She blocked out the busy restaurant with her eyelids. No way could she go through that again. And no way could she put Jack through it. He'd been too young to understand before, but he was reading so well now. What if he saw something on the front of a newspaper? She squeezed her jaw together. What kind of message was she giving to her son by lying to the world and letting Toby use her as a doormat? What kind of man would he become if this was his example?

'Oh, my God! It's Tobias Thornton! Can I have your autograph?'

Louise's eyes snapped open and she stared at two women hovering—no, make that *drooling*—next to Toby's chair. Toby smiled and did the gracious but smouldering thing his fans loved him for as he put his ostentatious squiggle on the woman's napkin. Louise just tapped her foot.

Only when they'd finished gushing and jiggling on the spot did they glance at her. And a split second scowl was obviously all she was worth. They didn't even bother keeping their voices down as they walked away. Huddled over her new treasure, she clearly heard one say, 'He is *so* hot!'

Toby opened his mouth to speak but, once again, his phone got the first word in. He glanced at the display, stifled a smile, then gestured to Louise that he was going to have to take this one. 'My agent,' he mouthed as he walked off to stand near the bar.

My foot, thought Louise, as the waiter cleared her half-eaten pasta.

She watched him out of the corner of her eye as he talked. Her husband smiled and laughed and absent-mindedly preened himself in the mirror behind the bar. His agent was male, over fifty and as wide as he was tall. No, Louise could do the maths. And the number she kept coming up with was *four*.

Even as something withered inside her, she sat up straighter in her chair. She demanded eye contact from Toby as he finished his call and sauntered back towards her. Now she got her smile— warm, bright, his eyes telling her she was the most wonderful thing in the world.

As he sat down at the table, he reached for her hand and brushed her knuckle with the tip of his thumb. Louise leaned forward and smiled back at him, turning on the wattage as only a former model knew how to do. And when Toby leaned in, clearly hoping he was going to be able to have his cake and eat it too this evening, she let the grin slide from her face and spoke in a low, scratchy whisper.

'Toby…' She paused, mentally adding all the names she wasn't about to call him out loud. 'I want a divorce.'

A hefty gust of wind blew up the river and ruffled the tips of the waves. The small dinghy rocked as Ben tied it to an ancient blackened mooring ring on a stone jetty. He stared at the knot and did an extra half-hitch, just to be sure, then climbed out, walked up along the jetty and headed up a narrow, stony path that traversed the steep and wooded hill.

He whistled as he walked, stopping every now and then just to smell the clean, slightly salty air and listen to the nagging seagulls that swooped over the river. At first glance it seemed as if he was walking through traditional English countryside, but every now and then he would pass a reminder that this wasn't a wilderness, but a once-loved, slightly exotic garden. Bamboo hid among the oaks and palms stood shoulder to shoulder with willows and birches.

After only ten minutes the woods thinned and faded away until he was standing in a grassy clearing that was dominated by a majestic, if slightly crumbling, white Georgian mansion.

Each time he saw this beautiful building now, he felt a little sadder. Even if he hadn't known its history, hadn't known that the last owner had been dead for more than two years, he would have been able to tell that Whitehaven was empty. There was something eerily vacant about those tall windows that stared, un-blinking, out over the treetops to the river below and the rolling countryside of the far bank.

He ambled up to the front porch and tugged at a trail of ivy that had wound itself up the base of one of the thick white pillars. It had been nearly a month since his last visit and the grounds were so huge there was no way he could single-handedly keep the advancing weeds at bay. Too many vines and brambles were sneaking up to the house, reclaiming the land as their own.

Laura would have hated to see her beloved garden's gradual surrender. He could imagine her reaction if she could have seen it now—the sharp shake of her snowy-white head, the determined glint in those cloudy eyes. Laura would have flexed her knobbly knuckles and reached for the secateurs in a shot. Not that her ar-thritic hands could have done much good.

At ninety-two, she'd been a feisty old bird, one worthy of such a demanding and magical place as Whitehaven. Perhaps that was why he came up here on the Sundays when it was his ex-wife's turn to have Jasmine for the weekend. Perhaps that was why he tended to the lilies and carnivorous plants in the greenhouses and mowed the top and bottom lawns. He stuffed his hands in his pockets and shook his head as he crunched across the gravel driveway and made his way round the house and past the old stable block. He was keeping it all in trust on Laura's behalf until the new owner came. Then he'd be able to spend his Sunday after-noons dozing in front of the rugby on TV and trying not to notice how still the house was without his whirlwind of a daughter.

He ducked through an arch and entered the walled garden. The whole grassy area was enclosed by a moss-covered red brick wall, and sloping greenhouses filled one side. It was the time of year that the insect-eating plants liked to hibernate and he needed to check on them, make sure the temperature in the old glass-houses was warm enough.

And so he pottered away for a good ten minutes, checking pots and inspecting leaves, until he heard a crash behind him. Instantly, he swung round, knocking a couple of tall pitcher plants off the bench.

The first thing he saw was the eyes—large, dark and stormy.

'Get out! Get off my property at once!'

She was standing, hands on hips and her legs apart, but he noticed that she kept her distance and worried the ends of her coat sleeves with her fingers. His hands shot up in surrender and he backed away slightly, just to show he wasn't a threat.

'Sorry! I didn't realise…I didn't know anybody had—'

'You're trespassing!'

He nodded. Technically, he was. Only up until a few seconds ago he hadn't known anybody cared—save a dead film star who'd loved this place as unconditionally as the children she'd never had.

'I made a promise to the previous owner, when she was ill, that I would look after the garden until the house was sold.'

She just stared at him. Now his heart rate was starting to return to normal, he had time to look a little more closely at her. She was dressed entirely in black: black boots, black trousers and a long black coat. She even had long, almost-black hair. And, beneath her heavy fringe, her face held a stark and defiant beauty.

'Well, the house has been sold. To me. So you can clear off now,' she said.

He pressed his lips together. There wasn't much he could say to that. But the thought of leaving Whitehaven and never coming back shadowed him like a black rain cloud. This new woman—striking as she was—didn't look like the sort to potter around a greenhouse or dead-head flower borders.

He picked up his coat from where it lay on the bench and turned to go. 'Sorry to disturb you. I won't come again.'

'Wait!'

He had almost reached the door at the end of the long, narrow greenhouse before she called out. He stopped, but didn't turn round straight away. Slowly, and with a spark of matching defiance in his eyes, he circled round to face her.

She took a few steps forward, then stopped, her hands clasped in front of her. 'The estate agent told me the place has been empty for years. Why do you still come?'

He shrugged. 'A promise is a promise.'

Her brows crinkled and she nodded. A long silence stretched between them, yet he didn't move because he had the oddest feeling she was on the verge of saying something. Finally, when she knotted her hands further and looked away, he took his signal to leave.

This time, he had his hand on the door knob before she spoke.

'Did you really know her? Laura Hastings?'

He let his hand drop to his side and looked over his shoulder. 'Yes.' A flash of irritation shot through him. For some unfathomable reason, he'd not expected this of her. He'd thought her better than one of those busybodies who craved gossip about celebrities.

'What was she like?' Her voice was quiet, not gushing and over-inquisitive, but her question still annoyed him.

He stared at her blankly. 'I really must be going. I meant what I said. I won't trespass here again.'

She ran after him as he swung the greenhouse door open and stepped out into the chilly October air. He could hear the heels of her boots clopping on the iron grating in the greenhouse floor. The noise echoed and magnified and he let the door swing shut to muffle it.

'Hey! You're going the wrong way!'

No, he wasn't. And he wasn't in the mood for chit-chat, either.

She didn't give up, though. Even though it must have been hell to stride after him in those high-heeled boots, she kept pace. Something to do with those long legs, probably. Either the changeable riverside weather had turned milder, or he could feel the hot anger radiating out from her as she closed the gap. He left the walled garden through a different gate from the one he'd entered by and chose a path that took him back down the hill towards his boat.

'I asked you to get off my land!'

He stopped and turned in one motion, and was surprised to find himself almost nose to nose with her. Not that she quite matched his six foot two, but she had the advantage of heels and a slight slope.

She stepped back but her eyes lost none of their ferocity.

He didn't have time for mood swings and tantrums. He had more than he could handle of those from Megan at the moment. That was why coming to Whitehaven was such a good distraction on a Sunday afternoon. It soothed him.

He looked Miss High-and-Mighty right back in the eyes. 'And I'm getting off your land as fast as I can.' Even though he had a strange sense that *she* was the trespasser. *She* was the one spoiling the peace and quiet of the one perfect spot in this world.

Her lips pressed together in a pout. One that might have been quite appealing if he weren't so angry with her for being here. 'The road is that way.' She jerked a thumb in the direction of the drive.

'I know.' He deliberately didn't elaborate for a few seconds. Just because he was feeling unusually awkward, although, in the back of his mind, he knew she was bearing the brunt of his frustration with someone else. But the woman in front of him was cut from the same cloth—exclusive designer cloth, by the look of it—and he just couldn't seem to stem his reaction. He took a deep breath. 'But my boat is tied up down by the boathouse.'

He blinked, waiting for more of her frosty words.

'I have a boathouse?' Once again, the tide had changed and she was suddenly back to being wistful and dreamy and far too beautiful to be real. That just got his goat even more. When she spoke again she was staring off into the bare treetops above his head. 'It's real? It wasn't just a film set?'

He shrugged and set off down the path and his features hardened as he heard her following him.

'Now what? I'm going, okay?' he called out, only half-turning to let the words drift over his shoulder.

'I want to see the boathouse.'

Ben normally loved the walk back down the hill on an autumn afternoon, but today it was totally ruined for him. He couldn't appreciate the beauty of the leaves, ranging from pale yellow to deep crimson. He didn't even stop to watch the trails of smoke snaking from the cottages of Lower Hadwell, just across the river. All he could hear were the footsteps behind him. All he could see—even though she was directly behind him and completely out of sight—was a pair of intense, dark eyes looking scornfully at him. It wasn't a moment too soon when he spotted the uneven stone steps that led down to the jetty.

As he reached the top step he heard a loud gasp behind him. Instinctively, he turned and put out a hand to steady her. But she hadn't stumbled. And she hadn't even registered his impulsive offer of help. She stood with her hands over her mouth and her eyes shining. Great. Now it was time for the waterworks. He was out of here.

As quickly as he could, he made his way to where his boat was tied and started untying the painter, busily ignoring her slow descent of the steps behind him. Just as he was about to step off the jetty and into the dinghy his mobile phone chimed in his back pocket. He would have ignored it, but it was Megan's ring tone. Something might have happened to their daughter.

And, since she was standing within reaching distance, not doing much but staring at the old stone boathouse, he slapped the end of the rope into the frosty woman's hands and dug around in his jeans pocket for his phone.

'Dad?' Not Megan, but Jasmine.

'What's up, Jellybean?'

There was a snort on the other end of the line. 'Do you have to keep calling me that? I'm almost twelve. It's hardly dignified.'

Ben's brows lowered over his eyes. Less than twenty-four

hours out of his custody and she was already starting to sound like her mother. 'What's up, Jas?'

'Mum says she can't drop me off this evening. She's got something on. Can you come and get me?'

Ben looked at his watch. Jasmine had been due back at five. It was past three now. 'What time?' Maybe it was just as well he'd had to leave Whitehaven early. It would take all of that time to cross the river, walk back to the cottage and drive the ten miles to Totnes.

He waited while his daughter had a muffled conference with her mother.

'Mum says she has to be out by four.'

Ben found himself striding along the jetty in front of the boathouse. 'I can't do it, Jas.' He kept walking while Jasmine relayed the information back to Megan. And when he reached the end of the jetty he turned and went back the way he'd come.

'Mum says she wants to talk to you.'

There was a clattering while the phone changed hands. Ben steeled himself.

'Ben? I can't believe you're being difficult about this! I know you've still got a soft spot for me, but it's time to let go, move on… This kind of behaviour is just childish.'

He opened his mouth to explain there was nothing *difficult* about not doing the physically impossible, but Megan didn't give him a chance.

'Everything always has to be on your terms, doesn't it? You'd do just about anything to sabotage my new life, wouldn't you?'

His voice was more of a growl than he'd intended when it emerged from his mouth. 'I do hope you are not letting our daughter overhear this. She doesn't need to witness any more arguments.'

Megan gave a heavy sigh. 'That's right. Change the subject, as always!' Still, he got the distinct impression she had moved into the hallway as her voice suddenly got more echoey.

'Megan, I'm at Whitehaven. This has nothing to do with

sabotage and everything to do with being too far away to get there by four o'clock.'

He waited. He could almost see the pout on his ex's face. And, as he found himself back by his boat, he noticed a similar expression on the woman standing there watching him. He abruptly turned again and carried on pacing. Not *exactly* the same expression. The lips were fuller, softer.

'Fine! Well, if you're too selfish to come and get her, I'll just have to take her with me. I'm having supper with…a friend. I'll drop her back at eight.'

And, with that, Megan ended the call. He was tempted to hurl his phone into the slate-grey waves. This was what that woman did to him—riled him until he couldn't think straight, until he was tempted to do foolish things. And he never did foolish things.

He jabbed at a button to lock the keypad, then stuffed his phone back in his pocket. Then he marched back to his boat.

'Thanks a lot for giving me some privacy,' he said dryly as he got within a few feet of the glowering woman on the jetty.

She gave him what his grandmother had used to call an 'old-fashioned look' and waved the rope she was holding from side to side. Incredible! How did the woman manage to make a *gesture* sarcastic?

'You didn't give me much choice, did you?' she said.

Ben ran his hands through his wind-tousled hair and made himself breathe out for a count of five. He had to remember that this wasn't the woman he was angry with, not really. 'Sorry.'

He'd expected the pout to make a reappearance, but instead her lips curved into the faintest of smiles. 'Divorced?'

He nodded.

'Me too,' she said quietly. 'That half of your conversation was giving me déjà vu. I bet I could fill in the blanks if I thought hard about it.'

Against his will, he gave half a smile back. 'You've got kids?'

'A boy,' she said, her voice husky. When she caught him

glancing up towards the house, eyebrows raised, she added, 'He's staying with his father while I move in down here.' She turned away quickly and stood perfectly still, staring at the woods on the hillside for a few long seconds.

When she turned back to him, a smile stretched her face. 'What do you know about the history of the boathouse?'

He played along. The same smile had been part of his wardrobe in the last two years. Thankfully, he was resorting to it less and less often. 'As far as I know, it was built long before the house. Some people say it's sixteenth century. And, of course, it featured prominently in the film *A Summer Affair*, but you know that already.'

The defiant stare vanished altogether and she now just looked a little sheepish as she stared at the glossy seaweed washed up on the rocks nearby. 'Busted,' she said, looking at him from beneath her long fringe. 'It was a favourite when I was younger and when I saw the details of the house, I knew I had to view it.' She turned to look back at the two-storey brick and wood structure. 'I didn't realise this place was real. I suppose I thought it was just fibreglass and papier mâché, or whatever they build that stuff out of…'

'It's real enough. I ought to…' Ben looked at the rope in his hand '…get going.'

She nodded. 'I'm going to explore.'

Ben stood for a few moments and watched her climb the steps up to a door on the upper level. It hadn't been used for years. Laura hadn't been steady enough on her feet to make the journey down the hill for quite some time before she'd died.

He climbed into the dinghy because it felt like a safe distance and carried on watching. The wooden floor could be beetle-infested, rotten. He'd just stay here a few moments to make sure the new owner didn't go through it.

His hand hovered above the outboard motor. Any moment now, he'd be on his way. He readied his shoulder muscles and brushed his fingertips against the rubber pull on the end of the cord. The loosened painter was gripped lightly in his other hand.

The boathouse was on two levels. The bottom storey, level with the jetty, had large arched, panelled doors and had been used for storing small boats. The upper level was a single room with a balcony that stretched the width of the building. He was waiting for her to walk out on to it, spread her hands wide on the railing and lean forward to inhale the glorious, salty, slightly seaweedy air. Her glossy dark hair would swing forward and the wind would muss it gently.

A minute passed and she didn't appear. He began to feel twitchy.

With a sigh, he climbed out of the boat and planted his boots on the solid concrete of the jetty. 'Are you okay back there?'

No response. Just as he was readying his lungs to call again, she appeared back on the jetty and shrugged. 'No key,' she yelled back, looking unduly crestfallen.

All his alarm bells rang, told him to get the hell back in the boat and keep his nose out of it. Whitehaven wasn't his responsibility any more. Only the message obviously hadn't travelled the length of his arm to his fingertips, because he suddenly found himself retying the boat and walking back up the jetty to the steep flight of steps that climbed up to the boathouse door.

As he reached the bottom step, she turned and looked down at him, one hand on the metal railing, one hand bracing herself against the wall. Her thick, dark hair fell forward as she leaned towards him.

'Do you know where the key is?'

With his fingernails, already dark-rimmed from the rich compost of the glasshouse plants, he scraped at a slightly protruding brick in the wall near the base of the stairs. At first, he thought he'd remembered it wrong, but after a couple of seconds the block of stone moved and came away in his hand. In the recess left behind, he could see the dull black glint of polished metal. Laura had told him about the secret nook—just in case.

He supposed he could have just told the woman about it,

yelled the vital information from the safety of the dinghy. He needn't get involved. Even now his lips remained closed and his mouth silent as he climbed the mossy stairs and pressed the key into the soft flesh of her palm.

There. Job done.

For a couple of seconds, they stayed like that. He pulled his hand away and rubbed it on the back of his jeans.

CHAPTER TWO

'THANK YOU,' she said, then shook her long fringe so it covered her eyes a little more.

She slid the key into the lock and turned it. He'd half-expected the door to fall open, but it swung in a graceful arc, opening wide and welcoming them in. Well, welcoming *her* in. But his curiosity got the better of him and he couldn't resist getting a glimpse.

'Wow.'

He'd expected shelves and oars and tins of varnish. Decades-old grime clung to the windows, and the filmy grey light revealed a very different scene. A cane sofa and chairs huddled round a small Victorian fireplace, decorated with white and blue tiles. A small desk and chair occupied a corner in front of one of the arched windows.

She walked over to the desk and touched it reverently, leaving four little smudges in the thick dust, then pulled her fingers back and gently blew the dust off them with a sigh.

'Did she come here often, do you know? Mrs Hastings?' she said, still staring at the desk.

Why exactly he was still here, keeping guard like some sentry, he wasn't sure. He should just go. He'd kept his promise to Laura. He wasn't required. And yet…he couldn't seem to make his feet move.

She turned to look at him and he shrugged. 'Not when I knew

her. She was too frail to manage the path down, but she talked of it fondly.'

She blinked and continued to stare at him, expressionless. He wasn't normally the sort who had the urge to babble on, but most women didn't leave huge gaping gaps in the conversation. He stuffed his hands in his pockets and kicked at the dust on the bare floorboards with the toe of his boot. Everything was too still.

'Not really the sort of place to interest a woman like you, is it?' he muttered, taking in the shabby furniture, the broken leg on the desk chair, held together with string. The place was nowhere near elegant enough to match her.

Her chin rose just a notch. 'What makes you think you know anything about what sort of woman I am?'

Just like that, the sadness that seemed to cloak her hardened into a shell. Now the room wasn't still any more. Every molecule in the air seemed to dance and shimmer and heat. She strode over to the large arched door in the centre of the opposite wall, unbolted it, threw the two door panels open and stepped out on to the wide balcony.

He was dismissed.

He took a step towards her and opened his mouth. Probably not a great idea, since during his last attempt at small talk he'd found a great muddy boot in it, but he couldn't leave things like this—taut with tension, unresolved. Messy.

Her hands were spread wide as she rested them on the low wall and looked out over the river, just as he'd imagined. The hair hung halfway down her back, shining, untouchable. The wind didn't dare tease even a strand out of place. He saw her back rise and fall as she let out a sigh.

'I thought I'd asked you to get off my property.' There was no anger in her tone now, just soul-deep weariness.

He turned and walked out of the boathouse and down the stairs to the jetty with even steps. She didn't need him. She'd made that abundantly clear. But, as he climbed back into the dinghy, he couldn't help feeling that part of his promise was still unfulfilled.

This time there were no interruptions as he untied the painter and started the motor. He turned the small boat round and set off in the direction of Lower Hadwell, a few minutes' journey upstream and across the river.

When he passed the Anchor Stone that rose, proud and unmoving, out of the murky green waters, he risked a look back. She was still standing there on the balcony, her hands wide and her chin tilted up, refusing to acknowledge his existence.

Louise had been staring so long at the field of sheep on the other side of the river that the little white dots had blurred and melted together. She refused to unlock her gaze until the dark smudge in her peripheral vision motored out of sight.

Eventually, when it didn't seem like defeat, she sighed and turned to rest her bottom on the railing of the balcony and stared back into the boathouse.

He couldn't have known who he'd looked like standing there below her on the steps as he'd offered her the long black key. It had been one of her favourite scenes in *A Summer Affair*—when Jonathan came to see Charity in her boathouse sanctuary, the place where she hid from the horrors of her life. Not that anything really *happened* between them. It was the undercurrents, the unspoken passion, that made it one of the most romantic scenes in any film she'd ever seen.

He had looked at her with his warm brown eyes and, somehow, had offered her more than a key as he'd stood there. For the first time in years, she'd blushed, then hurried to hide the evidence with her hair.

And then he'd had to go and spoil that delicious feeling—the feeling that, maybe, not all men were utter rats—by reminding her of who she was.

Louise stood up, brushed the dirt off her bottom and walked

back into the little sitting room. Of course, she wasn't interested in hooking up with anyone just now, so she didn't know why she'd got so upset with the gardener. Slowly, she closed and fastened the balcony doors, then exited the boathouse, locking the door and returning the key to its hiding place.

The light was starting to fade and she hurried back up the steep hill, careful to retrace her steps and not get lost, mulling things over as she went. No, it wasn't that she was developing a fancy for slightly scruffy men in waxed overcoats; it was just that, for a moment, she'd believed there was a possibility of something *more* in her future. Something she'd always yearned for, and now believed was only real between the covers of a novel or in the darkness of a cinema.

She shook her hair out of her face to shoo away the sense of disappointment. The gardener had done her a favour. He'd reminded her that her life wasn't a fairy tale—she snorted out loud at the very thought, scaring a small bird out of a bush. She was probably just feeling emotional because she wouldn't see Jack for two weeks. Toby had kicked up a stink, but had finally agreed that, once she was settled at Whitehaven, their son could live with her and go to the local school. She and Jack would be together again at last.

Toby had been difficult every step of the way about the divorce. Surprising that he would lavish so much time and energy on her, really. If he'd only thought to pay her that much attention in the last five years, they might not be in this mess at the moment.

She pulled her coat more tightly around her as she reached the clearing just in front of the house. The river seemed grey and troubled at the foot of the hill and dark woolly clouds were lying in ambush to the west. She ignored the dark speck travelling upstream, even though the noise of an outboard motor hummed on the fringes of her consciousness.

Not one stick of furniture occupied the pale, grand entrance hall to Whitehaven but, as Louise crossed the threshold, she smiled. Only two rooms on the ground floor, two bedrooms and one bathroom had been in a liveable state when she'd bought the house. All they needed was a lick of paint and a good scrub so she could move into them. The furniture would arrive on Wednesday but, until then, she had an inflatable mattress and a sleeping bag in the bedroom, a squashy, slightly threadbare floral sofa she'd found in a local junk shop for the living room, and a couple of suitcases to keep her going.

She'd let Toby keep all the furniture, disappointing him completely. He'd been itching for a fight about something, but she just wasn't going to give him the satisfaction. Let *him* be the one waiting for an emotional response of some kind for a change. She didn't want his furniture, anyway. Nothing that was a link to her old life. Nothing but Jack.

None of that ultra-modern, minimalist designer stuff would fit here, anyway. She smiled again. *She* fitted here. Whitehaven wasn't the first property she'd owned, but it was the first place she'd felt comfortable in since she'd left the shabby maisonette she'd shared with her father and siblings. She knew—just as surely as the first time she'd slid her foot into an exquisitely crafted designer shoe—that this was a perfect fit. She and this house understood each other.

The kitchen clock showed it was twenty past eight. Ben sat at the old oak table, a lukewarm cup of instant coffee between his palms, and attempted to concentrate on the sports section of the paper instead of the second hand of the clock.

Megan had never been like this when they'd been married. Yes, she'd been a little self-absorbed at times, but she'd never shown this flagrant disregard for other people's schedules, or boundaries, or…feelings. He wasn't sure he liked the version of Megan that she'd 'found'. Or this new boyfriend of hers that he wasn't supposed to know about.

Twenty minutes later, just as his fingers were really itching to pick up the phone and yell at someone, he heard a car door slam. Jas bounced in through the back door and, before he could ask if her mother was going to make an appearance—and an apology—tyres squealed in the lane and an engine revved then faded.

'Nice dinner?' he asked, flicking a page of the paper over and trying not to think about the gallon of beef casserole still sitting in the oven, slowly going cold. Eating a portion on his own hadn't had the comfort factor that a casserole, by rights, ought to have.

Jas shrugged her shoulders as he looked up.

'Just dinner, you know…' she said. And, since she was eleven-going-on-seventeen, he supposed that was as verbose as she was going to get.

'Have you done your homework?'

'Mostly.'

This was quality conversation, this was. But he was better off sticking to neutral subjects while he was feeling like this. In the last couple of years as a single dad, he'd learned that transitions—picking up and dropping off times—were difficult, and it was his job to smooth the ripples, create stability. Being steady, normal, was what was required.

'Define mostly,' he said, smoothing the paper closed and standing up.

Jas dropped the envelope of assorted junk she was clutching to her chest on to the table and threw her coat over the back of a chair. 'Two more maths questions—and before you say anything—'

Ben closed his mouth.

'—it doesn't have to be in until Thursday. Can I just do it tomorrow? Please, Dad?'

She stared at him with those big brown eyes and blinked, just once. She looked so cute with her wavy blonde hair not quite sitting right in its shoulder-length style. His memory rewound a handful of years and he could hear her begging for just one more push on the swing.

'Okay. Tomorrow it is.'

'Thanks, Dad.' Jas skirted the table and gave him a hug by just throwing her arms around him and squeezing, then she lifted a brightly coloured magazine out of the pile of junk on the table. 'Recreational reading,' she said, brandishing it and attempting to escape before he could inspect it more closely.

He wasn't so old that his reflexes had gone into retirement. The magazine was out of her fingers and in front of his face before she'd fully disentangled herself from the hug.

'What's this trash?'

Jas made a feeble attempt at snatching it back. 'It was Mum's. She'd finished it and she said I could have it.'

Ben frowned. *Buzz* magazine. He'd never read it himself, but he knew enough from the bright slogans on the cover that it was the lowest form of celebrity gossip rag. The lead story seemed to be 'Celebrity Cellulite'. Nice. What was Megan thinking of giving Jasmine a publication like this? Didn't his ex know how impressionable young girls were at Jas's age?

'I don't think this is appropriate.'

Jas rolled her eyes. 'It's interesting. All my friends read it.'

He raised his eyebrows. 'All of them?'

The nod that followed couldn't have convinced even Jas herself.

'That's what I thought,' he said. 'I mean, there's no substance in here. It's just rubbish…' He flicked through the pages, hoping his daughter would see what he saw. 'It's the worst kind of gossip. I—'

But then he stopped flicking idly through the pages, his whole frame frozen. His mouth worked while his brain searched for an appropriate sound. Getting a grip on himself, he carefully placed the magazine down on the table and stood, arms braced either side of it, as he stared again at the grainy photographs.

'Told you it was interesting,' Jas said with a smirk.

'But that's…'

Jas turned so she was side by side with him and leaned against his bunched-up arm muscles, looking down at the magazine too. 'Louise Thornton,' she informed him in an astoundingly matter-of-fact voice. 'Mum thinks she's a waste of space. Most people do.'

'Louise *who*?' he whispered hoarsely.

Jas punched him on the arm. 'Da-ad! You're stuck in the Stone Age! You know…She married Tobias Thornton—the actor.'

Who?

'We watched him in that action movie last weekend. The one with the bomb on the private jet?'

Oh. *Him.*

The picture was dull and not very clear—the product of a tele-photo lens the size of a space shuttle, no doubt. But there was no doubting the fierce glare in those eyes as she squared up to the paparazzo, her son clutched protectively to her, his face hidden. He'd been on the receiving end of that very same look just a few hours ago and it still gave him the shivers thinking about it.

'And she's famous?' he asked Jas, trying to sound as unin-volved as he actually was, but less involved than he felt.

Jas nodded. 'Well, famous for being married to somebody famous. That's all.'

Married. He should shut the magazine right now and condemn it to the recycling bin. Only…she'd said she was divorced. And, in the few moments that she'd let her icy guard down, he'd known she was telling the truth. The gaudy headline splashed across the top of the feature seemed to confirm his gut instinct: 'Louise's private hell since split!'

He took one last look at her image and felt a twinge of sympathy. Going through a divorce was bad enough, but having every spat reported for the world to see? More like a public exe-cution than a private hell. No wonder she'd freaked out when she'd found some strange man in her greenhouse.

He closed the magazine and looked at Jas. 'Sorry, Jas. I think these sorts of magazines are a gross invasion of privacy. I'd rather you didn't read it.'

She chewed her lip and her fingers twitched. He could tell she was torn between doing the right thing and insatiable curiosity. Thankfully, when she gave him a rueful smile and a one-shouldered shrug he knew he'd been doing an okay job of counteracting all the psycho-babble her mother had been subjecting her to since their separation.

He grinned. 'Good girl.'

Jas's smile grew and changed. 'Since I've earned a gold star, can I have fifteen pounds for a trip to the theatre with school?'

Ben looked heavenward. What was it with women and money? Any good deed seemed to need a reward—preferably in the form of shoes. Perhaps he should be glad that at least this was something educational. The shoes would come later. Oh, he had no doubt the shoes would come later. 'Give me a second while I find my wallet. What are you going to see, again?'

'The Taming of the Shrew.'

Ben nodded approvingly while he searched the kitchen worktops for his battered leather wallet. He hunted through the junk drawer. Where had he put the darn thing when he'd come in this evening? 'Jas, I'll come and give you the cash when I've found my wallet, okay?' he said, slamming the drawer in an effort to get it to close in spite of the disturbed odds and ends inside.

'Cool.'

'And Jas…?'

She turned at the doorway to the lounge.

'This Louise Thornton woman. Do *you* think she's a waste of space?'

She looked up at the corner of the ceiling and then back at him. 'Mum says any woman who puts up with that kind of…rubbish… and puts a man's happiness before her own is TSTL.'

TSTL.

'Too stupid to live,' Jas elaborated, knowing, as she always seemed to, when he needed a bit of help with her strange preteen speak.

The sounds of the television in the adjoining room accompanied his search for the wallet for the next ten minutes. He checked his coat, the car, the kitchen again… Just as he was racking his brain and replaying the day in his head, it struck him. He knew exactly where he'd left his wallet. He could see it so clearly in his mind's eye, he could almost reach out and touch it.

A rough wooden bench, long rays of the afternoon sun slanting through uneven Victorian glass. A black, soft leather square with cards and ancient till receipts poking out of it sitting next to a plant pot containing a rather spectacular nepenthes.

He sat back down on a chair and frowned. His wallet had been too bulky in the back pocket of his jeans and he'd taken it out and put it on one of the shelves in the greenhouse this afternoon. And then, with all the scowling and marching back down to the boat, he'd forgotten it.

He blew out a breath. If it had been just the cards and the few notes that were in there, he might have just left it. There was no way his face was going to be welcome back at Whitehaven any time this century. But the wallet contained one of his favourite photos of Jas and him together, taken in a time when she'd had ringlets and no front teeth and when he didn't seem to have permanent frown lines etched on his forehead.

There was nothing for it. He was going to have to go back.

Ben knocked on the door twice. Hard enough to be heard, but not so forcefully that he seemed impatient. And then he waited. The clear, pale skies of yesterday were gone and a foggy dampness dulled every colour on the riverbank. He turned his collar up as the mist rallied and became drizzle.

He raised his fist to knock again, but was distracted by a hint of movement in his peripheral vision. He turned quickly and stared at the study window, just to the right of the porch. Everything was still.

He grimaced and shoved his hands in his pockets. At least he and Louise Thornton were both singing from the same hymn sheet. Neither of them were pleased he was here.

Knowing she was probably hovering in the hallway, he knocked again, just loud enough to make a dull noise against the glossy wooden doors.

'Hello? I'm sorry for the intrusion—' He'd been going to say *Mrs Thornton*, but it seemed odd to use her name when she hadn't revealed it to him herself.

'I really didn't want to disturb you again,' he called out as he pressed his ear to the door, trying to detect a hint of movement inside, 'but I left something behind and I—'

There was a soft click as the door opened enough for him to see half of her face. She didn't have the heels on today—not that he ever noticed women's shoes—and, instead of being almost level with him, she was looking up at him, her face hard and unreadable.

'I left my wallet in the greenhouse,' he said with an attempt at a self-deprecating smile.

She just stared.

He should have looked away, ended the awkwardness, but she had the most amazing eyes. Well, eye—he could only see one at present. It wasn't the make-up, because this morning there was none of that black stuff. It wasn't even the hazel and olive-green of her irises, which reminded him of the changing colours of autumn leaves. No, it was the sense that, even though she seemed to be doing her best to shield herself, he recognised something in them. Not a familiarity or a similarity to anybody else. More like a reflection of something inside himself.

He shook his head and stared at his boots. This was not the time to descend into poetry. He had come here for one reason and one reason only.

'If you give me permission to retrieve it, I'll be out of your hair as soon as possible. I promise.'

She looked him up and down and then the door inched wider. 'Wait here and I'll get the key.'

A couple of minutes passed and Ben stepped out of the porch and on to the gravel drive, the crunch underneath his boots deafening in the still of the autumn morning. Louise Thornton reappeared just as he'd managed to find himself a spot where the pebbles didn't shift underneath him. Her long dark hair was scooped back into a ponytail, but the ever-present fringe left her face half-hidden. In her jeans and a pullover she *should* have looked like any other of the young mothers who stood outside the school gates.

He followed her up the hill, round the house to the top lawn. When she moved, her actions were small, precise, as if she didn't want to be accused of taking up too much space. Megan and all her friends had reached an age where their body language spoke of a certain confidence, a certain comfort in their own skin. This woman lacked that, despite her high-gloss lifestyle and multimillion-pound bank account.

Once again he felt an unwelcome twinge. He fought the urge to catch up with her, to tell her that it would get better one day, that there was life after divorce. But, since he wasn't exactly a glowing example of a man with an active social life, he thought it was better if he kept his mouth shut.

She unlocked the greenhouse door, then stood well back, giving him plenty of room to pass through. She didn't stay outside, though. He heard her footsteps on the tiled floor of the greenhouse behind him and, when he looked over his shoulder, she was watching him suspiciously.

The wallet was right where he'd remembered it was, tucked slightly out of sight next to a glossy carnivorous plant, groaning under the weight of its purple and green pitchers. He picked it up, jammed it into his jacket pocket, then stooped to pick up the saracenia that had been a casualty of yesterday's meeting. He'd forgotten all about it after Louise Thornton had appeared.

Carefully, he placed it back on the shelf and pressed the soggy compost down with his fingertips. Despite his ministrations, the slender pitchers pointed at an odd angle. He would have to bring a cane from home and…

No. There would be no canes from home. Not any more.

He stepped back and indicated the listing plant. 'This needs a cane. There might be one around here somewhere—' Down the other end was a likely place. He started to walk in that direction, checking behind pots and peering under the bench as he went.

'Why should you care?'

That kind of question didn't even warrant turning round to answer it. He carried on searching. 'It's a beautiful plant. It would be a shame to leave it to die.'

Once again he heard footsteps. Just a handful, enough for her to have stepped further into the greenhouse. He found what he was looking for—a small green cane—hidden between the windowsill and a row of pots. He picked it up, careful not to send anything else flying, and turned to find her fingering the delicate cream and purple foliage of the ailing saracenia.

'Then you really are a gardener?'

He moved past her, retrieved a roll of garden wire from a hook near the door and returned to the plant, unwinding a length as he walked. 'You think I like to play in the dirt for fun?'

She remained silent, watching him fashion a loop of wire wide enough to help the plant stand up without pinching it to the cane. When he'd finished, and the little plant was straining heavenwards once again, she took a few steps backwards.

'In my experience, most men are like big kids, anyway. So, yes, you may well be playing in the dirt for fun.' There was a dry humour behind her words that took the edge off them.

His lips didn't actually curve but there was a hint of a smile in his voice when he answered. 'It is fun. The earth feels good beneath my fingertips.' She raised an eyebrow, clearly unconvinced. He'd bet she'd never had dirt underneath her fingernails in her life. And he'd bet her life was poorer for it.

'Gardening gives you a sense of achievement.' He fiddled

with the stake and wire loop around the saracenia until it was just so. 'You can't control the plants. You just tend them, give them what they need until they become what they should.'

She broke eye contact and let her gaze wander over the plants nearest to her. 'These don't look like they're *becoming* much. Aren't you a very good gardener?'

He fought back the urge to laugh out loud. 'They're in their dormant phase. They'll perk up again, when the conditions are right.' He stood looking at her for a few seconds as she stared out into the gardens. 'Well, I've got what I came for. I'll be out of your hair now—as promised. I did say I was one not to break a promise, didn't I?'

He took a few long strides past her, breathed out and opened the greenhouse door. He was halfway across the lawn before she shouted after him.

'Then promise to come again.'

CHAPTER THREE

BEN didn't want to turn round. He'd told himself he wouldn't respond this time. After all, he'd had enough of high-maintenance women. But…

She stood on the lawn, watching him, her hair whipped across her face by another surly gust of wind. Once again, her eyes held him captive. Not for their dark perfection, but because something deep inside them seemed to be pleading with him. His friends had told him he was a sucker for a lady in distress, and he'd always denied it, but he had the awful feeling they might just be right.

She tugged a strand of chocolate-brown hair out of her mouth. 'The garden. It does need looking after. You're right. It would be a shame to…'

Once again, the eyes pleaded. He should have a sign made, reading 'sucker,' and just slap it on his forehead.

He'd do it. But not for her—for Laura. Just until he was sure this new owner was going to care for the place properly. And then he'd pass it on to one of his landscaping teams and charge her handsomely for the privilege. After all, he reminded himself, life was complicated enough already without looking after somebody else's garden.

Louise watched him go. She kept watching until long after his tall frame disappeared round the side of the house into a tangle of grass and shrubs and trees that were now, technically, her back garden. Not that she'd had the courage to explore it fully yet.

She forced herself to turn away and look back at the greenhouse.

Was she mad? Quite possibly.

In all seriousness, she'd just given a man she knew nothing about permission to invade her territory on a regular basis. Yet…there'd been something so preposterously truthful about his story and so refreshingly straightforward about his manner that she'd swallowed it whole. Next time she'd have to frisk him for a long-lens camera and a dictaphone, just in case.

She'd left the greenhouse door open. Slowly, she closed the distance to the heavy Victorian glazed door, with its beautiful brass handle and peeling off-white paint. On a whim, she stepped inside before she closed the door and stood for a few moments in the warm dampness. It smelled good in here, of earth and still air, but very real. She liked real.

The assorted plants lining the shelves by the windows really were quite exquisite. She'd never seen anything like them. Venus fly-traps sat next to frilly, sticky-looking things in shades of pink and purple. Then there were ones with large waxy leaves and bulbous pitchers the colour of ripe bruises. She walked over to the little plant that the gardener—Ben?—was that his name?— had saved. A thin green flute rose vertically, widening at the top with a frilly bit on top that looked a bit like a lid.

She felt an affinity with this little plant, recently uprooted, thin, fragile. Now in a foreign climate, reaching hungrily heavenwards with an appetite that might never be satisfied. She reached out and touched the damp soil at its base. It did feel good. She pulled her hand away, but didn't wipe it on the back of her jeans.

Near the door were the stubby brown plants that had started to hibernate. Just like her. All those years with Toby now seemed like a time half-asleep. Her mind wandered to a photo of a famous actress that had graced the pages of all the gossip magazines a few years ago. She'd been caught whooping for joy when the papers finalising her divorce had arrived. Since then she'd lost twenty pounds, received two Oscars and had been seen with a string of hot-looking younger men.

Shouldn't this be the time when *she* blossomed, came into her own? But it wasn't happening. She still felt dead inside.

Abruptly, she exited the greenhouse, closed the door behind her and marched back down the path to her new home. Once the house was sorted, she'd feel better. Only a few more days until the furniture arrived. Until then she could visit Dartmouth, the bustling town just a bit further down the river, and visit some of the art galleries she'd seen advertised. And she could find out what Jack would need when he started at the local school after the half-term holiday.

Yes, she'd definitely feel better when Jack could come here permanently. That was why she was feeling all at sixes and sevens. And he couldn't live here with a bedroom full of dust and cobwebs. He'd be here on the twenty-seventh of October—less than two weeks away. She clapped her hands together and smiled as she took a detour round the back of the house and entered through the back door. She had work to do.

Almost a fortnight later, Louise was putting the finishing touches to Jack's room. She looked at her watch. It was almost one o'clock, but she couldn't even contemplate eating anything. Only five more hours and Jack would be here. Her eyes filled with tears as she fluffed the duvet and smoothed it out, making sure it was perfect—not bunched up in the corners or with an empty bit flapping at one end.

It looked so cosy when she had finished that she flumped down on top of the blue and white checked cover and buried her head in the pillow.

Three weeks had been too long to go without seeing her son. She sighed. It had been the longest they had ever been apart. Toby had used to moan that she didn't travel with him any more, and maybe that had been part of the reason their marriage had crumbled. Even strong relationships were put under pressure when the couple spent weeks at a time apart. But how could she leave Jack? He was everything. He always would be everything.

It wouldn't have been fair to uproot him and ask him to change schools before the half-term break. She snuggled even further into the pillow, wishing it smelled of more than just clean laundry.

Toby had agreed—thank goodness—to let Jack live with her, even though they had joint custody. Her ex was away filming so often that it wouldn't have been fair to Jack to leave him at her former home in Gloucestershire with just a nanny for company. Even Toby had seen the sense in that.

So Jack would be with his father on school holidays and alternate weekends. And, just to appease Toby and make sure that he didn't change his mind, she'd consented to let him take Jack to stay in their—make that *Toby's*—London flat for the half-term week.

But tonight Jack would be coming to Whitehaven. He'd be here.

She turned to lie on her back and stared at the ceiling. She wasn't sure whether to laugh or cry. Mostly she just ached.

Minutes, maybe even half an hour, drifted past as Louise hugged herself and watched the light on the freshly painted ceiling change as the October wind bullied the clouds across the sky. Eventually, she dragged herself off the bed and sloped towards the window.

Something shiny glinted in the bushes and instantly her back was pressed against the wall, every muscle tense. After five seconds, she made herself breathe out. Nosing very carefully round the architrave, so only half of an eye and the side of her face would be visible from outside, she searched for another flash of light.

No-good, money-grabbing photographers! And trust one to turn up on the day Jack was due here. If she caught the…amoeba, she'd slap a lawsuit on him so fast his digital camera would fry.

In her effort to remain hidden, she only had a partial view of the front lawn. She remained motionless for some time, until her left leg started to cramp and twitch and then, only when she was very sure nobody was in her line of sight, did she lean out a little further.

Another glint! There!

Once again, she found herself flattened against the wall. But this time she let out a groan and slapped herself on the forehead. It wasn't a telephoto lens but a big shiny spade that had reflected the light. Ben the gardener-guy's spade. It was Sunday afternoon and he was here. Just as he'd been for the previous two weeks. Only she'd forgotten he'd be here today in all her excitement about Jack coming.

Not that she ever really saw him arrive when he came. At some point in the afternoon, she'd become aware that he was around. She'd hear him whistling as he walked up to the top lawn, or hear the hum of a mower in the distance.

So why had she felt the need to slam herself against the wall and pretend she wasn't here? This was stupid.

She stopped leaning against the wall and drew herself upright. There. Then she walked primly across the room and out of the door. No one was hiding. She was just walking around inside her own house, as she was perfectly entitled to do. Okay, she'd chosen a path across the room that had meant she couldn't have been seen from the window, but that didn't mean anything. It had simply been the most direct route. Sort of.

She found herself in the kitchen. It was in serious need of updating, with pine cabinets that had darkened to an almost offensive orange, but it had a fantastic flagstone floor and always seemed warm—probably because, in the now defunct chimney breast, there was an Aga. It looked lovely and spoke of families gathered in the kitchen sharing overflowing Sunday lunches, but she had no idea how to work it.

Well, that wasn't strictly true. She knew how to boil the kettle. And, at this present moment, that seemed like a shockingly good idea. She filled the battered old thick-bottomed kettle with water, lifted the heavy lid on the Aga hotplate and left the kettle to boil.

She hoped Jack would love it here as much as she did. What was she going to do if he decided he didn't like living in the depths of the countryside, far away from the flash mansion she'd shared with Toby? It was the only place he'd ever known as home. Well, that and the London flat. And the villa in Beverly Hills. Whitehaven was charming, but it lacked the gloss of her former houses.

She'd been getting what she needed out of the cupboards while she'd been thinking, and now discovered that she'd placed two teabags in two mugs. Something she'd done regularly in the early days after her split with Toby, but hadn't done for months now.

Her first instinct was to put the teabag and mug back in the cupboard, but that urge was hijacked by another one.

She might as well make one for Ben. She gave a short hollow laugh. It would be the nearest thing to payment she'd given him for all his hard work. The lawns were looking fabulous and, little by little, the shrubs and borders close to the house were starting to lose their wild look.

It wasn't that she hadn't intended to pay him. Just that she'd been heartily avoiding the issue. She'd acted like such a diva that first week, and she didn't know how to undo that all-important first impression. As if summoned up by her thoughts, she heard the crunch of footsteps outside. A moment later Ben passed the kitchen window, probably on his way up to the greenhouses.

A cup of tea seemed like a poor effort at a truce, but it was all she had in her arsenal at the moment. Boiling water lifted and swirled the teabag in the cup. Louise hesitated. Sugar, or no sugar?

On an instinct, she put one level spoon in the cup and stirred. He looked like a man who liked a bit of sweetness.

Another laugh that was almost a snort broke the silence. Well, she'd better have a personality change on the way past the herbaceous border, then. Especially if she was truly on a peace mission. At the moment she was the dictionary definition for the absolute opposite of 'sweetness'. *Meet Louise Thornton, sour old prune.*

When Louise arrived at the greenhouse, she realised she had

a problem. Two hands and two cups of tea meant that she had no spare limbs to open the door, or even knock on it. But it had seemed stupid to leave her mug of tea in the kitchen. By the time she'd delivered Ben's, discussed payment with him and walked back to the house, it would have been stone cold.

She peered inside the greenhouse and tried to spot him. The structure was long and thin—almost thirty feet in length and tucked up against the north side of the walled garden to catch as much sun as possible. Down the centre was the tiled path with wrought iron grating for the underfloor heating system. The side nearest the wall of windows was lined with benches and shelves, all full of plants, but on the other side large palms and ferns were planted in the soil at floor level.

Halfway down the greenhouse a leg was sticking out amongst the dark glossy leaves. She banged the door with her foot. The leg, which had been wavering up and down in its function as a counterbalance, went still.

She held her breath and tried to decide what kind of face she should wear. Not the suspicious glare he'd received on their first meeting, that was for sure. But grinning inanely didn't seem fitting either. In the end, she didn't have a chance to decide between 'calm indifference' and 'professional friendliness' because the leg was suddenly joined by the rest of him as he jumped back on to the path, rubbing his hands together to rid them of loose dirt, and looked in her direction.

She held up his cup of tea and then, when his face had broken into a broad grin, she breathed out. He was obviously really thirsty because he practically ran to the door and swung it wide. She thrust the mug towards him, ignoring the plop of hot liquid that landed on her hand as she did so.

He took it from her, smiled again and took a big gulp. 'Fantastic. Just how I like it. Thanks.'

Louise took a little sip out of her own chunky white mug. 'No problem. It's the least I can do.'

Ben leaned back against one of the shelves and took another long slurp of tea. He seemed completely at ease here. She tried to copy his stance, making sure she was a good five feet away from him, but she couldn't work out what to do with her legs and stood up straight again.

'Um… about payment…'

Ben raised his eyebrows.

'I can't let you go on doing all this for nothing.'

He shrugged. 'It started as a labour of love. I'm just sorry I haven't been able to do more.'

He wasn't making this easy. All she wanted to do was to work out what the going rate was and write him a cheque. She didn't want him to be nice. Men who were nice normally had a hidden agenda.

She put her mug down on the only spare bit of space on the shelf nearest her and drew herself taller. Only he didn't make that easy either. Her five-foot-eight wasn't too far away from his six-foot-plus height, but however much she straightened her spine, drew her neck longer, she still felt small beside him. But this was no time for weakness. She was the boss. She was in charge.

'Well, if you could just let me know how much you'd routinely charge for this sort of job…'

He drained his mug and looked at her with a more serious light in his eyes. 'I can't say any of my 'routine' work resembles this in the slightest.'

Louise crossed one booted foot in front of the other and a corner of her mouth rose. Oh, this was his game. Make it seem like he nobly didn't want anything, but sting her with an exorbitant price when it came to the crunch. And, if he played this game well, she was probably supposed to be shaking his hand and thanking him profusely for being so generous when the moment came.

She folded her arms, but only had to unfold them as he handed her back the empty mug.

'There's no rush for money. I'll send you a bill if you're really desperate for one, though.' He smiled, and it had none of the sharkish tendencies she'd expected after a conversation like that. 'Thanks for the tea.' And then he turned his back on her and returned his attention to a large plant with floppy leaves.

If there was one thing Louise didn't like, it was being ignored. It had been Toby's favourite way of avoiding anything he didn't want to talk about. All she'd had to do was utter the words, 'You're late. Where have you been?' and the shutters had come down, the paper had been opened and the television switched on. Nobody liked to be rendered invisible. She coughed and Ben looked up.

'No rush?' She'd promised herself she wouldn't be pushed around by any man again—ever. Okay, in her mind she'd meant *significant others*, but suddenly it felt important to stand her ground, to have this conversation on her terms. 'I'd much prefer it if we could talk figures now.'

He straightened again. 'Fine. It's just that I know you've just moved in, Mrs Thornton—' The pause was just long enough to indicate that he hadn't meant to say that. For the first time in their conversation he broke eye contact. 'I thought you might like a little more time to get settled.'

Louise felt her features harden. 'Why are you being so nice to me?'

Ben looked for all the world as if he hadn't a clue what she was talking about. Boy, he was good. She'd almost fallen for that straight-talking, man of the earth and sky nonsense. He knew who she was, and he wanted something from her. Maybe not money, but something. People always did.

Eventually he scratched the side of his nose with a finger. 'I suppose I felt I needed to make up for being a little…awkward… the first time we met. I was angry with someone else and I took it out on you. It's not something I'm proud of.'

A man who apologised! Now she *knew* the act was too good to be true.

Still, she was prepared to play along for the moment. He'd show his cards eventually. 'Well, if you're not going to be businesslike about this, I may just have to look in the *Yellow Pages* and find a gardener who is.'

He didn't seem that worried about losing her business; he just went back to fussing with the floppy plant. After a few seconds he looked back at her. 'Suit yourself.'

Once again, Louise felt as if she'd been dismissed. How dared he? This was her garden, her greenhouse. Those were her plants he was messing around with. 'At least give me your card.' That was a pathetic attempt at gaining control, getting him to give up something, but it was all she could think of.

He patted his pockets. 'I don't think I have one…ah!' He pulled his wallet out of his back pocket and rummaged around inside. The card he pulled out was creased and the edges were soft. She took it from him and backed away.

Oliver Landscapes. Very grand for a one-man band outfit.

'Feel free to let me know if you don't want me to come any more, but if I don't hear any differently, I'll just assume I should just pop by again next Sunday.' This time he didn't turn away and continue working; he just looked at her. Not with barely concealed curiosity, or envy, or even out-of-proportion adoration. Those kinds of responses she was used to. No, this was something different. He looked at her as if she were transparent.

She didn't know what to do.

'Just come,' she said and fled, leaving her mug of lukewarm tea in the shade of a wilting ficus.

Louise couldn't help grinning as she climbed out of the car, even though the weather was disgusting and she was about to get on a tiny ferry and cross an angry-looking river. Just as well she could see their destination—the village of Lower Hadwell— only a few minutes away on the opposite shore.

The rear door opened and Jack climbed out, tugging at the collar of his new school uniform and looking a little uncomfortable. He was tall for his age and he had his father's good looks.

Half the class at his previous school—the female half—had cried for a week when he'd told them he was moving away.

Not that Jack cared. He had no idea that his golden blond shaggy hair was anything but a nuisance to comb in the mornings. He might have Toby's physical characteristics, but he lacked any of his father's swagger. And long may it stay that way. Louise knew from first-hand experience just how devastating a weapon all that beauty mixed with a little too much confidence could be.

'All ready to go?'

Jack nodded and clutched his book bag. Louise wanted to take his hand and hug him to her. He was being so brave. Starting a new school was difficult for any kid, but Jack was going to face an extra set of challenges. She'd had a meeting with the head-mistress to discuss it and they'd both decided that, quietly, the word would go round that Jack was to be treated like every other child in the school. He wouldn't get any favours, but he shouldn't be subjected to endless questions about his dad or expected to buy the whole class shed-loads of sweets, just because his parents were rich.

She laid a reassuring hand on his shoulder. Jack was a normal boy in that he wouldn't allow public displays of 'soppiness'.

At this time in the morning there were regular ferries across the river and they walked to the edge of the high stone jetty and waited for the little wooden boat, painted white with a blue trim, to sputter up to a seaweedy flight of steps.

The ferryman paid them absolutely no attention other than to take coins off them and Louise breathed a sigh of relief. Lower Hadwell was a small community and news of her arrival in the area had to have spread. She just hoped they were all like this guy. Completely uninterested. And, with that blissful thought in her mind, she sat on the hard wooden bench that circled the stern of the boat and turned her face into the wind.

By the time they reached the jetty on the other side of the river, she was sure her hair had picked up a bucket-load of salt that was blowing up the river from the sea. Never mind. She'd deliberately dressed down in a tracksuit and baseball cap, hoping she'd blend in a bit more with the other mums at the school gate.

Jack declared the boat ride 'wicked' and jumped out of the ferry in one smooth motion. Louise followed, although her clamber on to dry land was nowhere near as graceful.

The school had to be at the top of the steepest hill in the whole of south Devon. Oh, my goodness! Louise's calves begged for mercy as they trudged past a pub, cottages in hues of cream and earthy pink and a handful of shops. Jack stopped and turned round to face the river.

She grabbed on to his coat and tried to inhale enough oxygen to talk. 'Jack!' The noise that came out of her mouth barely registered as a croak. 'Come on!'

Jack gave her his usual I'm-eight-and-I-understand-the-universe-much-better-than-you look. 'Try walking backwards. It doesn't hurt so much.'

Louise couldn't work out if that was the most sensible idea she'd heard in years or the most stupid. She stared at her son as he started ascending again, this time with his backpack pointing up the hill. Heck, she'd do anything to stop the fire in her calf muscles. She did a one-eighty and followed suit. Her legs fairly sang with relief.

This was much better! At least it was until she came unexpectedly into contact with something tall and warm. Something that went 'oof'. Louise squeezed her eyes shut, yelled an apology and turned and ran up the hill after Jack, who had made much better progress.

Coward, she thought, as she reached the level ground just outside the school gates. But it was only a minute before the bell was due to go and she didn't need someone recognising her and delaying her by asking for an autograph or something.

Jack stopped just short of the wrought iron fence around the quaint village school. Louise bent over and tried to suck in more air. She knew from the furnace in her cheeks that her face was probably pink and blotchy and sweat was making her back feel all sticky.

She laid an arm on Jack's shoulder—more to support herself than anything else. She went to the gym every now and then. So why had this finished her off?

The jangle of an old-fashioned brass school bell rose above the screams and shouts of the playground. She stood up, put a hand on each of Jack's shoulders and stared into his eyes. 'You ready?'

Jack pressed his lips together and nodded just once. She grinned at him and, as she spoke, she turned to walk through the gate.

'Then it's show t—'

A bright flash seared her retina. At first she couldn't work out what had happened, but the guy who jumped out from behind a parked car with a whacking great camera round his neck kind of gave it away. Instinctively, she pulled Jack to her and started to run. She really, really wanted to swear, but this was neither the time nor the place.

As they reached the safety of the school building, all grey stone and arched windows, she started to chastise herself. She'd been stupid not to have been prepared for this! Of course the tabloids would want a picture of Jack starting at his new school. They were desperate for any titbit about either her or Toby. And, while Toby had gushed at length about the new love in his life, she'd steadily maintained her silence.

Jack was in tears. And it took a lot to make her little man cry.

Louise marched up to the school reception and fought back tears herself while she waited for the receptionist to stop fiddling with the photocopier. Maybe she should just have given an interview to *Celebrity Life* or something. Her refusal to play their game had just made incidents like this inevitable.

Jack was hugging on to her, his face buried under her armpit. She stroked the top of his hair.

Now she was good and angry. She and Toby were fair game.

They'd chosen this life. But Jack had no choice. When she'd got her son settled in, she was going back outside and she would find that photographer and she would shove his camera so far down his throat that he'd be coughing up bits of his memory card for weeks.

CHAPTER FOUR

BEN was happily walking down the road, minding his own business. Well, almost. He'd just spotted a picture of the Wilkinsons' cottage in the estate agent's window and was actually paying more attention to that than the direction in which his feet were heading. He and Megan had dreamed about buying that cottage for years.

With his current income and the maintenance payments to Megan, could he afford it? Maybe.

But, before he could do the mental arithmetic, he was winded by some idiot charging up the hill backwards.

He didn't even have the chance to say *hey!* before the track suited figure garbled out an apology and ran off.

Hang on a minute! He *knew* that idiot!

He was so busy staring up the hill at the pink-clad bottom with the word *'Juicy'* emblazoned across it that he was almost knocked over a second time by a man in a large anorak and a wild look in his eyes. He had a huge camera in his hand.

Ben shrugged. Bit late in the season for bird-watching, but what the heck did he know? Global warming was having a weird effect on the wildlife in this area. Last year some strange-looking bird only seen in the isles of Scotland had been blown down to the south coast of England by a freak storm. The local 'twitchers' had gone bananas. That man had had the same crazed look in his eye. Marauding ornithologists aside, nothing was going to stop him from wandering down to the newsagent's and get his morning paper before his meeting today.

However, Mrs Green, owner of the shop for the last thirty-three years and purveyor of local gossip, was in a chatty mood. Ben valiantly attempted to tuck his paper under his arm and drop the money in her hand, but her arms stayed firmly folded across her ample chest and he was forced to hover, one hand reaching over the counter, as the inquisition began.

'I heard that another celebrity has bought Whitehaven, Mr Oliver. What do you think of that?' She narrowed her eyes and analysed his reaction. He was trying hard not to have one. Something might have given him away because she added, 'Of course, I expect you know all about that—having been so friendly with Laura Hastings and all.'

'I just helped out in the garden, really.' He waved the coins again, hoping the glint of something shiny might distract her.

'Yes, but you'd know if the place had been sold, wouldn't you?'

'Not necessarily.' He didn't know why he was protecting Louise Thornton. Just that, having been the source of local gossip himself a few years ago, he knew how unpleasant, how…invaded… it could make one feel.

'Well, whoever it is…' Mrs Green leaned back and looked down her nose at him; it made him feel like a slice of something on a glass slide under a microscope '…they'll be fine with the residents of Lower Hadwell. After all, we've been used to living with a bona fide Hollywood legend on our doorstep for the last twenty years, haven't we?'

He nodded and thrust the money at her again. This time he wasn't going to be put off. Just as she started to uncurl her hand to accept it, she paused and nodded in the direction of the magazine rack that was half-hidden by a tall shelf containing pet food and assorted stationery. 'That mag that your Jasmine was waiting for has come in. I expect you'll be wanting to pick that up as well.'

Ben's mouth straightened into a thin line. He stuffed the coins back in his coat pocket and retreated to the safety of the other side of the shop, pleased that he was hidden by the boxes of envelopes balanced on the top shelf.

Now was it *Pink!* or *Girl Chat* that Jasmine liked? One had a free lip gloss with it, and he wasn't sure about that, so he picked up the other one.

There was a sudden jangle of the shop door and a rush of cold air. A figure slammed the door closed and darted behind the shelving unit to join him.

'Louise?'

She pulled the baseball cap she was wearing further down over her eyes and crouched a little lower. 'Shh!' she whispered loudly, without looking at him. Then she froze and slowly turned her head to look over her shoulder. 'Ben?'

He didn't say anything back. It was obvious who he was.

'You're wearing a suit,' she said, forgetting to hunker down.

Just then the wild-looking ornithologist appeared, running down the street. Louise must have seen a hint of movement out of the corner of her eye, because she practically flattened herself against the shelves, sending a box of ballpoint pens flying. 'Did he see me?' she hissed at him, looking a little wild-eyed herself.

Ben tried to look nonchalant and peered out of the shop window, but it was difficult to see clearly with all the posters for local events and cards offering bicycles for sale and adverts for paperboys.

'I think he's gone.'

Louise edged closer to where he was standing and craned her neck. 'Are you sure?'

He nodded. 'He was going at some speed when he shot past here. On a hill this steep, it's pretty difficult to stop when you've built up that kind of momentum. Why are you worried about—'

Oh. If Jas had been in his shoes she would have slapped herself on the forehead and said *duh!* Paparazzi. Definitely not a species seen around Lower Hadwell before. It put a totally new spin on the whole 'invasion' issue.

'Couldn't you just let him have a picture and then he'd be on his way?' That seemed like a reasonable solution.

Louise looked at him as if he'd just suggested she do a nude photo-shoot on the jetty—in sub-zero temperatures.

'I'm so…flipping cross with him, I might not be responsible for my actions. He just scared the life out of Jack as we were on our way into school.'

Her son was here? Good. Perhaps then she'd lose that slightly haunted look from her eyes. The look that unwittingly begged him to rush in and be her knight in shining armour. His armour had gone into retirement when he'd signed his divorce papers, and he'd better remember that fact.

She sighed and straightened up a little. 'A photo of us looking shocked is bad enough, but a shot of me turning pink in the face and spitting obscenities at him would only stoke the fire. By Friday there'd be a whole pack of them camped out at the local inn waiting for us.' She rubbed her face with her hand. 'Thank goodness I'd calmed down enough to realise that when I spotted him following me again.'

She stopped talking and looked him up and down. 'You're wearing a suit. A very nice suit.'

'You already said that.'

'Won't it get dirty?'

'Nope.'

She glowered at him. 'Stop being obtuse.'

He was tempted to chuckle, but decided it wouldn't help her current mood. 'I know you think I'm only fit for weeding the flower beds, but actually I'm not a gardener by trade. Not exactly.'

Louise's mouth dropped open. A sensation of achievement swelled inside him. Although why he should feel so stupidly proud of the fact that *he* was bamboozling *her* for a change, he wasn't sure.

'I'm a landscape architect. I design outside spaces—town centres, open spaces, parks, private homes. This morning Lord Batterham, the owner of the large stately home near here, wants to chat to me about restoring a knot garden on his estate and building an environmentally friendly play area for visitors.'

She blinked. Twice. And closed her mouth. 'Oh.'

She seemed to have forgotten all about the photographer, which had to be good news, so he decided to keep her distracted. 'You look a little different yourself.' Gone were the elegant clothes in dark, muted tones, replaced by a baby-pink tracksuit and bright white running shoes. And what was the cap with the ponytail sprouting through the back all about?

'I look a mess,' she muttered.

He took in her appearance again, went beyond the surface impression. Her face was free of make-up and her cheeks rosy with fading anger. A slightly more dishevelled appearance suited her. It made her more approachable…touchable.

He took a step back.

'Every day for months I've not gone out without my best clothes or my make-up on. Trust some rat with a digital camera to turn up when I'm looking…well, less than perfect.' She shook her head. 'I swear they must have some kind of radar to target me on my off days.'

'You look fine.'

She tipped her head to one side and gave him a weary look. 'I think what you said was that I looked "different". Believe me, it spoke volumes.'

'I just meant…not your normal self.'

That's right, Ben. Just dig yourself in deeper.

He was bad at this kind of stuff, he knew. He didn't have the ability to dress words up and make them pretty. And what was so wrong with the plain, unvarnished truth, anyway?

'Not my normal self?' she said, staring hard at him.

He sighed inwardly. Megan hadn't appreciated his 'lack of

tact and incredible insensitivity' either. Some women were just too much hard work.

'Well, here's your explanation…' She pulled a magazine off the rack and thrust it in front of his face. It took him a few moments to realise that the blurry picture on the cover was Louise herself—playing catch on a beach with a little boy. But that wasn't all. The caption read 'Celebrity Bulges' and large red lines circled her tummy and thighs.

He snatched the magazine from her and slapped it back in the rack, upside down and with the cover facing inwards. She locked him with a steady gaze and, when she spoke, her voice was low and dry.

'Apparently, I've been letting myself go. I'm surprised you hadn't heard.'

Her ability to mock herself blind-sided him. Laughter rocked him from the inside and burst out of his mouth. And then, after a few seconds, she joined him. Her eyes widened, as if she was as surprised at her own response as he was.

It was kind of surreal to be huddling in a little country newsagent's, hiding from the press and chortling with Louise Thornton. The laughter subsided to a level where he could get a bit of control and he wiped his hand over his face.

Louise was no longer laughing, but she was still smiling. If the topic of conversation was transformations, here was one that beat them all. The remains of his laughter died away instantly.

She was truly beautiful when she smiled. Her eyes sparkled and her skin glowed. Why did she think she needed all that black stuff to make her look pretty? He almost wished the photographer was here right now to capture this moment.

Thinking of cameras and lenses, he walked to the shop window and looked up and down the street. 'No sign of him now. I think you're safe.'

Louise's brows changed shape as she frowned, then relaxed again. The smile vanished and the remote beauty returned. 'Of course.' She stood up properly and started picking up the pens scattered all over the floor. When she'd finished, she gave him another smile, but this time her eyes were unaffected. 'I'll see you on Sunday?'

He nodded.

'I promise I won't make you weed the flower beds, if you're really too grand for that.'

It was his cue to laugh again, but he couldn't bring himself to. 'I've been itching to sort that garden out properly for years. Just indulge me, okay?'

She nodded. And, although she was as collected and self-contained as always, he could see a hint of something in her eyes. As if she wanted to reach out but was too afraid.

'I promise I'll charge the earth and drink all your tea.'

That earned him a real smile. Small, but real.

'It's a deal, Mr Landscape Architect.' She looked at her watch. 'Speaking of which, didn't you say you were off to a meeting?'

Lord Batterham!

He hurried back to the counter to pay Mrs Green for his paper. She was standing there, holding a magazine in her hand—the same one Louise had flourished in front of his nose. She stared at it and then at Louise, and then back at the magazine cover, as if she were playing some kind of mental tennis match.

For the first time in thirty-three years she wasn't making a sound. He plopped the change in front of her on the counter, grabbed Louise by the hand and dashed out of the shop.

'Mum? Can we go outside? It's stopped raining.'

Louise stopped herself from putting the kettle on the Aga for a fifth time. She didn't really want another cup of tea. It was just that, at some point this afternoon, somebody might.

'Can we? Please?' Jack's voice was so high-pitched on that last word she was sure dogs would be bounding towards them from all over the district.

'Can we *what*?'

Her son ran to the back door and opened it, letting in a gust of damp November air. Louise walked over to where he stood and stuck her head out of the door. Moisture dripped from the leaves of an evergreen bush in the little courtyard directly outside the kitchen, but the clouds were now a pale, pearly grey and she even thought she saw a hint of blue before it was hurried away by the wind.

Fresh air would do her good. Fresh air would stop her waiting. Or wondering why he was late. Well, not late, because they'd never really set a time for him to come and go, but later than normal.

She shook her head and reached for the scarf and hat on a peg nearby. Ben Oliver had turned all her assumptions about him on their heads once this week already. Why shouldn't he do it again?

The grass on the sloping lawn in front of the house was still damp, but it didn't stop Jack deciding a game of football was the ideal way to burn off a bit of energy. They used a couple of the big stones lining the driveway to mark out the goals.

She'd never been good at games at school, always too tired from acting as surrogate mother to her four younger brothers and sisters and part-time carer to her invalid father. Jack was running rings around her but then he misjudged a kick and the ball went flying past her towards the edge of the woods. She ran after it and stopped it with the side of her boot. If all went according to plan, she would have at least one goal to Jack's seven by the time they gave up and headed back inside for hot chocolate.

She swung her leg in an almighty kick. A jarring pain hit her as her lower back met something flat and solid and, all of a sudden, she was staring at the sky. She could hear Jack laughing his head off some distance away.

'Just you wait!' she yelled, giggling slightly herself, but the mirth stopped when she attempted to move. 'Ouch!'

'Here.' The voice was as rich as dark chocolate and she recognised it instantly. She also recognised the broad, long-fingered hand that came into her field of vision—although exactly when she'd noticed the shape of Ben Oliver's hands, she wasn't sure.

Even through the wool of her gloves, his skin was warm and he gripped her hand in such a way that she knew she could give him all her weight and he wouldn't let her fall. She winced as he gently helped her to her feet. 'Ow.'

'Where does it hurt?'

She didn't want to draw even more attention to her slightly-larger-than-planned and somewhat muddy backside. 'Where d'you think?'

'Do you want me to take a look?'

'No!' She twisted out of his grip and brushed herself down, more for something to do than for cosmetic effect. 'Don't tell me you're an almost-doctor as well as an almost-gardener.'

He laughed and she looked up at him, her irritation dissolving. It was only then that she noticed the girl standing slightly behind him. She had shoulder-length, honey-coloured hair, nothing at all like Ben's dark mop, but her eyes were all her father's.

Ben grabbed his daughter's hand and pulled her forward a little. She blushed and looked at the ground. 'Louise, I'd like you to meet my daughter, Jasmine.'

'Nice to meet you, Jasmine. I'm Louise. Your dad's been helping me out with my garden.'

'I know.' The reply was barely a whisper, and Jasmine flushed an even deeper shade of red.

Her father may not have known who 'Louise Thornton' was the first time he'd met her, but Jasmine certainly did. This kind of reaction wasn't unusual. Heck, she'd been just the same when she'd started going out with Toby and he'd introduced her to the latest Oscar-winning Hollywood actress.

'Come and meet my son, Jack. He's football mad, I'm afraid, though.'

Jasmine shrugged and followed her across the lawn as Ben strolled along, bringing up the rear. Jack took one look at Jasmine and Louise knew he'd decided she was okay. As the child of a celebrity couple, he had an uncanny kind of radar for discerning between hangers-on and real friends. He made instinctive decisions in a second and he was rarely wrong. Now, how did she go about getting herself some of that?

Jack picked up his football and started walking in the direction of the back door. 'There's chocolate cake inside. Want some?'

Jasmine nodded furiously and broke into a trot to keep up with him as he raced off towards the kitchen.

Ben fell into step beside Louise as they followed their offspring. 'Sorry I had to bring Jas with me. I hope it's okay.'

'Of course it's okay. Who do you think I am? The wicked witch of the West?'

He was smirking when she looked up at him. 'You can be a tad fierce at times.'

Was she? Really? She fell into silence for a few seconds while she pondered his remark. What had happened to the shy, sweet Louise she'd once been? Where was the awkward girl with the too-long limbs and a school blazer that had been far too short?

Eventually, she said quietly, 'If you'd been really afraid, you wouldn't have come.'

Ben laughed again. She liked that sound. She wondered if she could make him do it some more. So far, it had only happened accidentally, when she hadn't actually been trying to be funny at all.

'True. I hadn't intended on bringing Jas at all. It's just that…' he ran his hand through his hair '…it's complicated.'

'Trust me. I know *complicated*. What's up?'

Ben stared off into the distance for a few seconds and she stopped walking, aware that it would be better if this conversation wasn't overheard from the kitchen. Ben halted beside her.

'My ex-wife, Megan…' He made a microscopic movement with his head, as if he wanted to shake it but was stopping himself. 'She's a good mother, really. It's just that lately her priorities have been a little skew-whiff.'

Louise nodded.

'She seems to think that, now Jas is almost in secondary school, she can fend for herself a bit more. And, probably, she could. It's just with the divorce still in the recent past, I think Jas feels a little neglected. Megan had last-minute plans and cancelled their Sunday afternoon together. I don't think she even realises how shut out Jas feels sometimes.'

'How long?'

'Since the divorce? Two years.'

'Two months for me. Although I kicked him out about a year ago.' Louise breathed in. 'Girls need a mother at that age.'

She had certainly ached for her mother, going through those awkward years, but Mum had died just as she'd been on the brink of puberty, and she'd had to muddle through on her own. At least, when her sisters had reached it, she'd been able to help them along.

Maybe if Mum had been around she wouldn't have been quite as dazzled by Toby. Not that Toby hadn't loved her at first. It was just that he wasn't a good long-term choice. A little motherly advice would have come in mighty handy.

After years of looking after everyone else in the family— paying the bills, cooking the meals, wiping noses and changing bedpans—it had been like a fairy tale. A rich, handsome young man had arrived on the scene to take her away from all that. What seventeen-year-old girl wouldn't have jumped at the chance?

'Well, Jas is very welcome here. I understand completely.'

For the first time since she'd met him, she felt as if she wasn't a complete mess compared to him. Ben gave a small smile and looked at the ground. 'Thanks. Anyway, there's not much light left. I'd better get started.'

Jack started yelling his question as he ran down the hallway, finishing it as he skidded into the kitchen in his socks. 'Jas says there's fireworks on tonight. Can we go?'

Fireworks? Oh, of course. Time had taken on a strange quality since she'd moved to Whitehaven. The date was… what? The second or third of November? It was only days away from Guy Fawkes night and there would be bonfires and firework displays all over the area this weekend. She'd thought the bangs she'd distantly heard last night must have been shotguns, but now it all made sense.

'I don't know, Jack. What time is it? And where?'

'I'll ask Jas!' He raced out of the kitchen before she could quietly explain that maybe it wasn't such a good idea to be out in public, that maybe the Olivers wouldn't want a couple of extras tagging along. She fiddled with her cup of tea while she waited for her son to return but, after a couple of minutes, she decided he must have found something else to get all hyper about and had lost interest.

They didn't need to go out to see fireworks. Whitehaven was perched high on a hill and there would be great views from the attic windows. They could watch at a safe distance.

Ben knocked softly on the back door. There was no reply. He stared at the chunky Victorian handle for a second, then gripped it, the brass chilly against his palm, and turned. The door swung open on surprisingly creak-free hinges.

'Hello?'

Louise was standing at the old butler's sink, staring out of the window. He could hear water sloshing and see bubbles splashing and a moment later she dumped an upturned cup on the draining rack. It fell over. She didn't even look at it, just grabbed the next bit of crockery off the pile and started washing again. He coughed.

All the sloshing and splashing stopped. She didn't alter the angle of her head, but somehow he could tell that her focus was no longer off in the distance. She was aware of him, he knew. And, somehow, that made him aware of her too.

Suddenly, she started washing the plate she was holding again. When it must have been scrubbed clean of every last speck of food, she placed it on the drying rack with exquisite care, then turned to face him, wiping the bubbles off her hands with a tea towel.

'All finished?'

He nodded.

A million snatches of small talk whizzed round his head, but meaningless words weren't his forte. And Louise didn't seem to require any. She gave him a look—not quite a smile, more an expression of openness, of welcome—and then filled the kettle. He breathed a sigh of relief.

When he'd been married to Megan, he'd got used to having an arsenal of such phrases for the moment when he'd walked through the door. She'd always needed him to say something, to pay her attention, to make her feel noticed. And he'd adapted, because she was his wife and it had been what she'd needed.

Louise motioned for him to sit at the chunky kitchen table and started rummaging in a cupboard. After what he'd seen the other day, he wouldn't have been surprised if *this* woman was thoroughly fed up with being noticed, so he did nothing to break the wonderful stillness that surrounded her. He just drank it in and slowly felt his muscles relax. She handed him a mug of tea, sweetened to perfection, then pottered round the kitchen.

Rampaging children, however, could not be counted on to be so restful. Jas and Jack stormed into the kitchen just as the last knot was about to ease from his shoulders.

'Mum, I'm hungry!'

Even when she smiled, wide and full, as she was doing now, she still had a sense of elegance and poise that he'd rarely seen. At first he'd thought it was standoffishness, although it was merely reserve, but he could understand how people who perceived her to be an attention-hungry bimbo could misinterpret it as snobbishness. Louise Thornton was indeed an intriguing mix of contradictions. He was curious to know more.

'You're always hungry,' she said, looking at her son.

'Can we have some cake? Pleeeease? After all, we've got guests.' Jack looked hopefully at Ben and Jasmine, and Ben chuckled. Having been a hollow-legged boy once himself, he was pretty sure Jack's request wasn't entirely altruistic. However, he wasn't about to talk himself out of a nice piece of cake, so he watched for Louise's reaction.

She rolled her eyes and pulled a large tin off the counter. It was the item she'd been rummaging for earlier. Clever woman. She'd been prepared.

When she opened the lid the most delicious waft of treacle and walnuts, reminding him of warm November evenings by the fire, hit him. He almost had to wipe the drool from his mouth with his sleeve by the time a large chunk was handed to him on a plate. He didn't waste any time doing it justice.

Now, he could make a decent casserole and a great roast dinner, but baking evaded him entirely. This must be a prize-winning, locally made example. As he bit into it, he was almost tempted to growl with pleasure.

Light, moist cake with dense, spicy flavours and the earthiness of walnuts teased his taste buds. Almost half the slice was gone already. Would it be rude to ask for another one? He looked over at Jack, who had cleaned his plate, but was wearing a significant amount of crumbs over his face and down his front. Now, there was a lad who could be counted on to ask for more. All Ben had to do was hop on the bandwagon when the opportunity came.

Jack opened his mouth and Ben swallowed his last mouthful, confident that his plate would not lie desolate for long.

'So, can we go to the fireworks, Mum? Please?'

Louise frowned and put the lid on the cake tin. Ben felt his shoulders sag.

'I don't know, Jack. I thought we could watch from upstairs. That way, we might get to see more than one display.'

Jack pursed his lips. 'Jas says there's going to be hot dogs on the village green. Can't we go and have hot dogs?'

She looked pained as she shook her head. 'I'm sorry, darling. After the way that photographer… Well, it's just better we stay here where no one will see us.'

Jack's face fell and Louise's was a mirror image of misery. Ben wished there was something he could do. It was criminal that a mother and son couldn't do something as simple as watch a firework display without being hounded. He remembered only too well how hard he'd had to work not to stay inside every evening and mope when his divorce had been fresh and raw. With the extra pressures on Louise, he could see her turning into a hermit.

Jack slumped forward on the kitchen table, his chin in his hands and his bottom lip sticking out. Ben stared at the wall straight in front of him, racking his brain for a solution. Slowly, the pegs containing hats and coats and scarves near the back door came sharply into focus. He stood up.

'I've got an idea.'

CHAPTER FIVE

THE other three stopped talking and looked at him. He grinned, walked over to the row of pegs and pulled off a fluffy knitted hat and matching scarf. 'Come with me,' he said as he walked back towards Louise, whose eyes were wide and round, then he linked the tips of his fingers with hers and pulled her up to stand.

Her mouth moved, but no sound emerged.

He tugged her in the direction of the hallway, to the large gilt mirror he'd seen hanging there on his very first visit after Louise had moved in. He stood behind her and, while she continued to stare at him in the mirror, he pulled the dusky purple hat over her head. It was one of those tight-fitting ones with no embellishment or bobbles, and the crocheted hem came down level with her eyebrows.

Better. But she still looked like *Louise Thornton*. He scowled at her reflection and her eyebrows raised so they disappeared under the hat. It was the hair. That long, glossy dark hair was her trademark—instantly recognisable, indefinably *her*.

He brushed the hair framing her face back behind her ears and twisted the strands into a loose plait. When his gaze flicked up to the mirror again, she was staring at their reflections, her mouth slightly apart, and then she shivered and shook his hands away from her shoulders. He broke eye contact and busied himself wrapping the scarf once, twice, around her neck, letting it stand up so it covered the lower half of her face. Somehow his hands had made their own way back on to her shoulders with the flimsy pretence of keeping the scarf in place.

Only the eyes gave her away now, but there wasn't much he could do to diminish their impact. She could hardly wear sunglasses on a chilly autumn evening. That would only draw more attention to her.

'There.'

She was motionless, the only movement her eyes as they flicked between her own reflection and his. 'I'm wearing a hat and scarf. Is that your stunning plan?'

'No one will be able to pick you out of a crowd in this. It's going to be almost pitch-dark, after all. Top it off with a big dark coat and you'll look just like the rest of us.'

'I *am* like the rest of you.'

He knew celebrities weren't a different breed of human being, so he could almost agree. But there was something about Louise Thornton that defied explanation, that made her unlike anyone he had ever met before. And he really hoped he didn't feel that way because she was famous. He didn't want to be that shallow.

They stared at each other in the mirror a good long time. Her shoulders rose and fell beneath his hands.

'Mum, look!'

The stillness was shattered and suddenly he was moving away and Jack and Jasmine were running into the hallway, bundled up in coats and hats and jumping up and down. Jack was tall for his age and Jasmine petite, making them almost the same height. It took a few seconds for him to realise that Jack's overexcited squeaking was coming from underneath Jasmine's hat and scarf. Louise looked from one child to the other and burst out laughing. She pulled the fluffy hat with earflaps up by its bobble until she could see her son's eyes.

'If you'd have kept quiet, I'd have had no idea that you two had switched coats!'

Jack jumped up and down. 'Can we go? Can we?'

Louise rolled her eyes again. 'Okay, we'll go.'

Their cheers echoed round the tall hallway and up the elegant sweep of the stairs. Pounding footsteps followed as they raced back into the kitchen. 'You can wear your own coats and hats, though,' Louise called after them.

When the silence returned, she looked at him. 'Do you really think it'll work?'

'Of course, everyone is going to be craning their necks and looking up at the sky. They won't even pay attention to who's standing next to them. And, let's face it, it has to be a better disguise than your last attempt!'

She pulled the hat off her head and spent a few seconds de-fluffing her hair. 'You don't beat around the bush much, do you?'

He shook his head. Why waste time using inefficient words when you could use a few that hit straight to the heart of the matter?

Louise unwound the scarf and held it, together with the hat. 'Was it really that bad?'

He nodded and tried very hard not to smile. 'You looked like a celebrity trying very hard to *not* look like a celebrity. I mean, a pink track suit with the word "*Juicy*" splashed all over the…um…back.'

She gave him a knowing look. 'Oh, you noticed that, did you?'

If Ben Oliver had been a man prone to blushing, he'd have been as pink as Louise's '*Juicy*' jogging bottoms at that moment. Thank goodness his body was far too sensible for such displays of emotion. He gave her the sort of look a headmaster would give a gum-chewing schoolgirl. 'It was hard not to.'

'When are the fireworks going to start?' Louise looked first to the left and then to the right and clung a little harder on to the rope strung between rusting metal poles in front of her. Lower Hadwell's village green bordered the river just upstream from the main jetty and the fireworks had been set up on the stony beach with a clear boundary marked out to stop excited children getting too close.

'Twenty minutes.' Ben's voice was calm and reassuring, but it did nothing to soothe her. 'Don't worry.' His hand rested lightly on her shoulder and she jumped.

Don't worry. That was easy enough to him to say. Every time he let his guard down, someone didn't jump in front of him and pop a flashbulb. In recent years, she'd stopped letting down the wall she put up between herself and the rest of the world. Life was just too dangerous to lay herself open in that way. Only now the tabloids labelled her 'stuck-up' and 'fake'.

She sighed and, as her warm breath flowed out of her mouth, cool night air laced with wood smoke and sulphur filled her nostrils. She smiled.

Her family—well, what had been left of her family once Mum had died—had always attended the little firework display in the local park each November. The fireworks themselves hadn't been all that spectacular, but her memories were of cosiness, laughter and a feeling of belonging.

Then she'd met Toby and all that had changed. Had her family life really been that bad? On paper…probably.

As the eldest of five, with an invalid father, she'd had to fill her mother's shoes. The role had been too big for her. Like a little girl playing dressing up in her mother's high heels, there'd been obstacles she just hadn't been able to negotiate. In her dramatic teenage way, she'd imagined herself as a modern-day Cinderella—albeit looking after a much-loved family. She'd become cook, cleaner, carer, sympathetic ear, referee…

But what their lives had been lacking in money and glamour, they'd made up for with love. And she hadn't realised all families weren't like that until there was a big gaping hole in her life.

'Mum? Can I have a hot dog?'

Louise blinked and then focused on Jack, who was tugging on one of her arms.

'Pardon, sweetheart?'

He tugged so hard she thought her shoulder would work loose from its socket. 'I'm really hungry. Can I have a hot dog?'

The smell of onions, caramelising as they cooked on the makeshift grill on the far corner of the green invaded her senses. Hot on its tail was the aroma of herbs and meat. Her nose told her that when Jack said 'hot dogs' he didn't mean skinny little frankfurters but bulging, meaty local sausages, bursting out of their skins and warming the soft, floury white bread that surrounded them. Her mouth filled with saliva.

'Jack, you're going to pull my arm off! Give me a second to think!'

She was safe here at the front of the crowd. No one could see her face, only half lit from the bonfire off to the left. But over there by the grill, a generator grumbled as it provided power for a couple of harsh floodlights, making it as bright as any runway she'd ever walked down when she'd been modelling.

'Um...'

Ben took hold of Jack's hand, his eyebrows raised in a question as he searched her face. 'Why don't we let your mum save our spot here and we can go and get the hot dogs? If that's okay with you...' he added a little more quietly.

Her face relaxed so much in relief that she couldn't help but smile. She nodded and almost breathed her response. 'Thank you.'

It was only when Ben and the two kids had disappeared through the crowd that she realised she should have asked him to get one for her too. She opened her mouth to yell, but stopped herself and pulled the hem of her hat down until it was touching the bridge of her nose. Too many faces.

There were always too many faces these days. Yes, back in the beginning, she'd loved that aspect of her golden life with Toby. Dad had needed a lot of help when she'd been finishing secondary school and, after being in class so infrequently that some of the kids in her year hadn't even known who she was, it had been nice to be recognised. She'd underestimated just how addictive being noticed could be.

Her first hit had been the adrenaline rush she'd had when that talent scout for a modelling agency had come up to her when she'd been working in the supermarket one Saturday afternoon. Within weeks she'd been flying round Europe for photo shoots, attending industry parties, meeting famous people…

Dad had been so proud of her. And she'd ignored the guilt she'd felt at letting Sarah, the next oldest, slip into her Cinderella role whilst her big sister had danced away in an imaginary world where the clock never seemed to strike midnight.

And then she'd met Prince Charming—Tobias Thornton, rising star and darling of the British film industry. After that, she'd smothered all those nagging feelings by reasoning that now, at least, her family had decent food on the table. That they'd moved into a proper house with a bedroom for all of them… except Louise. And the school uniforms were no longer hand-me-downs or scavenged from local charity shops. Best of all, Dad had a full-time nurse to look after him.

It had been the nurse who'd been sitting beside him when he'd died only six months after she and Toby had said 'I do' on a private island in the Caribbean.

Tears stung Louise's eyes and the bonfire became a big orange blur. She stared at the mass of colour until it started to sharpen and move again. Slowly, she became aware of people talking and being nudged, but she didn't seem able to move. It was only when she heard Jack laugh and splutter with a mouthful of hot dog that she realised the others had returned. She carelessly rested a hand on top of Jack's head but he shook it off.

'You looked hungry too.' There was a smile in Ben's voice and she turned to look at him, even though the world was still shimmering slightly. He was holding up a big, juicy sausage in a roll, dripping with fried onions and ketchup. 'Of course, I've heard models don't eat, so I'm prepared to make the sacrifice of eating two if you don't want it.'

'Ex-model,' she said, snatching it out of his hand and stuffing one end in her mouth before he could change his mind. Ben threw his head back and laughed. And, when she had finished chewing, she did the same.

'Mum? What's so funny?'

Louise gave a tiny shake of her head, her gaze locked with Ben's. 'I don't know, Jack. Just…' Ben was still grinning, but his eyes weren't just smiling at her now. Deep underneath, there was something intense, something that drew her and terrified her at the same time. '…something.'

She breathed out and returned her attention to her hot dog, which wasn't hard to do. She hoped these had been happy pigs because, boy, they made one heck of a good sausage. Their sacrifice had been entirely worth it.

But then, sacrifices often were.

If Mum hadn't died, if Dad hadn't been ill, if she hadn't been standing at that particular supermarket till that day—looking 'haunting' as the scout had told her—then she wouldn't have met Toby. Okay, she might not have any regrets about erasing Toby from her life at this particular moment, but without Toby there would have been no Jack. And Jack was worth any sacrifice.

She looked at him, hanging off the rope and trying to edge closer to where the fireworks were being set up. Before she could reach for him, a strong male hand gently grabbed his coat and hauled him back into place.

A bonfire sprang into life inside Louise. In a place that had been cold and dead for so long, flames licked and tickled.

No. Not now. Not here. Not with this man.

Not that Ben Oliver wasn't worthy of admiration. After all, he was good-looking, thoughtful and kind. A good father. All the things a girl should put at the top of her list when searching for a prospective Prince Charming. And he had a presence, a quiet charisma that made it impossible not to search him out in a crowd or feel that he was someone you could trust your life with.

But this wasn't the time to be noticing those things about someone. This was time for her and Jack to heal, to rebuild. And she'd felt this way before, had trusted Toby with her life, and he had made it glitter and shine for a while, but ultimately he'd decided it wasn't worth his enduring attention.

So this was her sacrifice: she wouldn't go there. She'd cut off the oxygen supply to whatever feelings were warming her core. Jack deserved all her attention and her love at the moment and he shouldn't have to share it with anyone. He wouldn't.

The fireworks started. Louise had thought herself immune to the pretty showers of colour. Last year they'd seen the New Year's fireworks in London from a balcony of an expensive riverside apartment a quarter of a mile away. It had been a dramatic display, with rockets shooting off the London Eye and barges on the Thames, but she'd felt removed from it all somehow.

There was no ignoring anything tonight. Not the way the crowd collectively held its breath waiting for a bang. Not the warmth of the bonfire on one side of her face. Especially not the breath of the man standing slightly behind her that made her right ear tingle.

In the inky blackness of a country night, the sprays of light—from pure white to red and green, and blue and gold—were reflected in a river that had stretched itself taut and flat. The effect was stunning. Magical. Soon she was saying 'ooh' and 'aah' with everyone else, and clapping and watching Jack's reaction—and finding herself catching the gaze of a warm brown pair of eyes, then quickly looking away again.

The last firework glittered and fizzed, shooting so high up into the sky that she would have sworn that, briefly, she caught a glimpse of her big white house on the opposite bank. And then it exploded and split into a thousand stars that gracefully fell to earth. She sighed and closed her eyes. Simple pleasures.

How odd. She'd always thought that money and fame would make it easier to find pleasure, but all it had really done was make it more complicated. Pure happiness, joy with no strings attached was an unknown commodity in her life. When had she become so poor? And how had she become so blind she hadn't even realised what a sorry state she was in?

'Come on…' Ben's hand, resting once again on the shoulder of her thick wool coat, caused her to open her eyes, releasing the magic moment and letting it flutter away like the sparks from the bonfire. 'I'll give you a lift home.'

Jack, who should have been totally worn out by now, jumped up and down even harder. 'Are we going on the dingy again?'

Jas put on a very superior tone. 'It's not a dingy, Jack. You say it *ding-gee*. Dinghy.'

Jack pulled himself up to his full height. 'I knew that.'

Ben shook his head. 'No. I'll drive you.'

Louise opened her mouth to protest. It would take more than half an hour to drive down to Dartmouth, catch the 'higher ferry', as the locals called it, and double back to Whitehaven.

'I wouldn't take the kids out in the boat when it's this dark,' he explained.

Louise followed him as he headed for the quiet spot where he'd parked his car and looked carefully at the scenery. It had been verging on darkness when they'd made the trip over, or at least she'd thought it was. The trees had been dark grey shapes and the sky had faded from bright cobalt at the horizon to indigo overhead but, compared to how it looked at the moment, that had merely been twilight. Everything was black if it wasn't lit up by either starlight or electricity.

'And you and Jack would have to scramble back through the woods in the pitch-dark.'

Okay, he'd convinced her. She got lost in her own back garden in daylight still. No way was she dragging her eight-year-old through those woods tonight.

As she strapped Jack into the back of Ben's car, Louise went still. Ben must have known all along that they wouldn't be able to return to Whitehaven the way they'd come. It explained why he'd disappeared when they'd first arrived to move his car—away from the main road and the village centre, where the crowds were now ambling—into a quiet side road.

She sat in the front passenger seat and fastened her seat belt without looking at him. Pretty soon they were whizzing through isolated country lanes in silence, the only hint they weren't alone inside a big black bubble were the golden twigs and branches picked out by the headlights in front of them. The patterns the light made on the road and hedgerows shifted and twisted as they sped past. Every now and then, for a split-second, an odd tree stump or a gate would be illuminated and then it would be gone.

Louise breathed in the silence. After a few minutes she turned her head slightly to look at Ben. His hands gripped the wheel lightly, but she had no doubt he was in full control. All his concentration was focused on the road in front of them. He looked at it the same way he'd looked at her in the mirror that afternoon.

The air begun to pulse around her head and a familiar craving she'd thought she'd conquered started to clamour deep inside her—the heady rush of simply being *noticed*. Immediately, she twisted her head to look straight ahead and clamped her hands together in her lap. They were shaking.

Simple pleasures.

She had an idea that Ben Oliver was full of them.

It was taking every ounce of his will-power to keep his eyes on the road ahead. Having Louise Thornton in the front seat of his car was proving a distraction. And not an oh-my-goodness-there's-a-celebrity-in-my-car kind of distraction. Unfortunately. He could have talked himself out of that one quite easily.

And it wasn't even because she was the most stunning woman

he'd ever laid eyes on. She was way out of his league, he knew that. The logic of this situation would catch up with him eventually.

At the start of the evening, she'd stood tall and still, and a casual onlooker would have thought her relaxed and confident. But, unfortunately, he'd discovered he could no longer regard Louise casually.

He'd noticed the way her gloved hands had hung on to the boundary rope as if it were a lifeline. He'd seen the panic in her eyes when she'd thought she'd have to face the crowd and might be recognised. He had the oddest feeling that the real Louise had shrunk small inside herself, hiding beneath the thick outer shell. How long had she been that way?

Then, as the evening had worn on, he'd seen her hands unclench from the rope and noticed the unconscious, affectionate gestures that flowed between mother and son. He'd heard her laugh when ketchup had dripped on to her chin from the hot dog, and listened to the soft intakes of breath with every bang and crackling shower of the fireworks.

And he didn't want to notice these things about her. He didn't want to know how warm and rich her laugh was, or how tender and gentle she was below the surface. He just wanted to see the surface alone—much in the same way he only saw the rippling surface of the river and never the rocks and currents beneath.

He would rather remember the bare facts—that her divorce was still raw and fresh, that the last thing he and Jas needed in their lives at the moment was another woman with too much baggage for him to shoulder.

He'd known that Megan had had 'issues' when he'd first met her, but they seemed inconsequential to the situations facing Louise. And she faced them with such dignity and poise…

There he went again, admiring her when he should be concentrating on other things.

A flash of movement across the road caused his foot to stamp instantly on the brake. All of the joke-telling and giggling from the back seat stopped.

'It's okay,' he said, his heart pounding. 'Only a rabbit—and he's away up the hill by now.'

Jas and Jack returned to their knock-knock jokes and he put the car into gear. He pulled away gently, aware of the slim fingers that had flown to the dashboard and were now curling back into her lap.

Getting freaked out by a rabbit? What was happening to him? They darted in front of the car all the time and he never usually reacted this way. He pressed his foot on the accelerator, the car picked up speed and soon they were flying down the country lane as if nothing had happened. Ben concentrated on the road and pretended he didn't know how to answer his own question.

The other occupants of the car fell into silence and it wasn't long before he was pulling into the long drive that led to Whitehaven. Louise shifted in her seat, as if she was preparing to dart out of the door as soon as the wheels had stopped turning. Good. If she didn't feel the need to linger in his presence, that was fine by him.

'Can I have cake when I get in, Mum?'

Ben stifled a smile as he slowed the car and brought it to a halt outside the front porch. And then his tummy rumbled. It had fond memories of that cake.

'Jack! It's past your bedtime! Of course you're not going to have—'

'Cakes!'

They all turned and looked at Jas, whose eyes were wide and a hand was clamped over her mouth. Then she started to cry. Instantly, he was out of the car and opening the rear passenger door. 'Jas? What is it?'

Jas's lip trembled. 'C-cakes. My class are doing a tea party for the old people in the village. Mum was going to help me make cakes this weekend, but she went away…'

Ben tried not to let the irritation show on his face. Megan

could waltz off to Timbuktu for all he cared, but when her flaky ways affected Jas it was a different matter entirely.

'I'm supposed to take them in on Tuesday morning or I won't get any house points!' Jas wailed. 'Can you help me, Dad?'

'Um…' There was nothing he'd like more, but he wasn't sure Jas would be getting any house points for anything he tried to bake—'tried' being the operative word.

'I can help.'

As one, he and Jas swivelled round to look at Louise and stared. Her face was expressionless. Had he really heard that right?

Ben turned back to Jas. 'Can't you do it on your own? I'll supervise.'

There was a loud snort from the passenger seat. He ignored it.

Jas had the end-of-the-world expression on her face that was common to all eleven-year-olds in a crisis. 'I don't know. I can never get the beginning bit right when you have to mix the eggs and flour together.'

'Eggs and sugar.' Louise spoke quietly. In his experience, that tone was deceptive. He just might be in big trouble.

'Yeah, eggs and sugar. That's what I meant,' Jas said absently.

Ben sighed. 'Can't we just buy some?'

Jas shook her head and started to cry again.

'I can help.' This time Louise's tone was more insistent.

'Home-made cakes?'

'What do you think you were eating earlier? Scotch mist?'

Reality dropped away and Ben felt as if he were standing on nothing. '*You* made that cake?' He could tell by the look on her face that he was probably sabotaging Jas's only chance—which was a pity. He hadn't meant his words to come out quite like that, but they'd escaped before his brain had had a chance to give them the once-over.

Louise glared at him. 'No, the cake fairies left it on the doorstep.'

Okay. He'd deserved that.

Jas, who was wiping her eyes with her coat sleeve, piped up.

'I thought that if Jack needed cakes for school you'd have just bought them at Harrods.'

It seemed his daughter had inherited his capacity for opening his mouth only to change feet.

Louise clamped a hand across her mouth and, just as he was expecting her to flounce out of the car, slamming the door, her eyes sparkled and she let out a raucous laugh.

Ben was floored. This wasn't the shy giggle he'd seen earlier; it was a full-bellied chuckle. And it was pretty infectious. When the surprise had worn off, his mouth turned up at the corners and, pretty soon, all four of them were crying with laughter. Louise was clutching on to the door for support and Jack's titter was so high-pitched it was starting to hurt his ears.

Still giggling, Louise managed a few words, even though she was a little short of breath. 'Sometimes…sometimes…when I was really busy…I *did* get them at Harrods!' That just set them all off again.

When they all managed to get back on the right side of sanity he felt as exhausted as if he'd done a cross-country run. Man, it hurt to breathe.

Louise let out a long happy sigh. Her face was soft and relaxed and her cheeks were flushed. It was just as well there were two children in the back of the car, because he had the stupidest urge to kiss her.

That sobered him up pretty fast.

'Are you sure? I know you're really busy. We don't want to put you out, do we, Jas?'

Jas didn't say anything, but pleaded at him with her eyes.

'Busy doing what?' Louise raised an eyebrow. 'The house is practically finished. There's only so much interior decorating a girl can do, you know.' And then she winked at him—actually winked at him. 'I'd be happy to help. You gave us a great night out tonight.'

Ben stuttered. That was the problem. In his mind, tonight had been about making a nice final gesture to ensure that Louise was settled into the neighbourhood before he backed off. How was he going to do that if she was going to be in his kitchen tomorrow?

After she'd put Jack to bed that night, Louise couldn't sleep. Didn't even want to try. It must be the fresh air or something.

She found herself flopped on one of the big velvet-covered sofas in the drawing room, the remote control in her hand, flicking through endless cable stations searching for something to watch. A fire glowed in the hearth and the lights were low. The rich, deep colours and luxurious textures of the fabrics in here truly had made a large draughty room incredibly cosy.

Wait a minute...

She stopped jabbing the button on the remote and went back a few channels. Just as she'd thought—there was old film footage of Laura Hastings, not from one of her movies, but of her getting on a plane. Louise dropped the remote and snuggled back into the over-sized cushions that lined the back of the sofa.

It was obviously a documentary and, although she'd missed the first twenty minutes, she settled down to watch. Laura had been so beautiful when she was young. Her ice-blonde hair, pale skin and blue eyes looked fabulous in gaudy nineteen-fifties Technicolor.

She'd had such an interesting life. Two failed marriages—a hint of a scandal. Louise smiled to herself. It all might seem very dashing and glamorous when it was reported like that, but she knew from experience that living through it was just as painful as it was for the rest of the human beings on the planet. Not only did she admire the former owner of Whitehaven, but she identi-fied with her. Had Laura Hastings been happy in the end?

As she kept watching, she didn't really get an answer. Laura had lived life to the full, taken every chance offered her. And that was where Louise saw the difference between them. Yes, she'd grabbed at the chance to become a model and marry the man of her dreams—literally. But then, even when things had turned sour, she'd hung on to the empty shell of all her hopes, too scared to let go and trust that things would turn out right in the end.

Her gaze drifted from the television and she huffed gently and shook her head. She'd been a coward. It had taken Toby carrying on, practically under her nose, to push her into leaving him. She'd been scared that, imperfect as it was, if she let go of her life she'd go into freefall and there'd be no one there to catch her.

She still felt as if she were falling sometimes.

A picture of Whitehaven appeared on the screen and Louise sat up. Wow. The footage looked like old black and white cine film. Laura, now middle-aged but still stunning, walking on the lawn in front of the house, staring out across the river.

Much more of the house was visible. The trees were, of course, shorter but it wasn't just that. Everything looked a little more... cared for. The garden still had a wild and unusual beauty, but there was a harmony that was missing from it in its present state.

The house and garden might have been looking lovely, but the voiceover indicated that Laura Hastings's life had been disintegrating at this point. She'd fallen in love with both the house and her leading man while filming on location at Whitehaven some ten years earlier.

There had been a torrid affair, but the actor already had a wife and Laura had married someone else on the rebound. Years later, the illicit romance had blossomed into life again and Laura, sure that happiness was finally in her grasp, had divorced her husband and waited for her lover to free himself from his marriage too. The waiting had turned into yearning and the yearning into heartbreak. The love of her life had never followed through.

A tear trickled down Louise's cheek and she hugged a pillow to her. Laura Hastings might have made some bad choices along the way, but she couldn't help admiring her courage.

The credits rolled. The next thing on was *A Summer Affair*, the very film set at Whitehaven. It was the story of the young serving girl who'd captured the heart of the wealthy owner's son. The chemistry on-screen between Laura and her man was sizzling-hot. But, now Louise knew it had ended in a doomed love affair, every touch, every kiss had a bittersweet quality to it.

She sighed and settled down to watch, a chenille cushion hugged to her chest.

There was a scene halfway through the film, just as the lovers were starting to act on their feelings for each other, that had been filmed on the balcony of the boathouse. A picnic was set out on a little table with a red and white checked cloth. The sun was shining and shy, heated glances were flying between hero and heroine.

Louise sighed. That was what love should be like, she mused as she covered her mouth with a hand to stifle a yawn—overly bright and colourful, the sun always shining. The zing of electricity in the air. And the way he looked at her—as if he could see right through her and into her soul. As if he wanted to drown in her. That was what love *should* be like.

What a pity it was only like that in corny old movies, she thought, as the hero pulled the heroine into the shadowy interior of the boathouse and wrapped her in his arms.

CHAPTER SIX

Louise's eyes were closed. A gentle summer breeze warmed her skin and she could hear the waves half-heartedly lapping against the jetty below the balcony. She let out a long therapeutic sigh, stretched her legs and opened her eyelids.

The sky was the colour of cornflowers and the sun a glaring dot of white gold high above.

'Perfect timing.' The male voice was warm and lazy, and accompanied by the dull pop of a cork exiting a wine bottle. 'I thought you were going to sleep all afternoon.'

She shook her head and stood up. The chequered red and white cloth on the small table fluttered, lifted by the warm air curling in and out of the boathouse balcony. Self-consciously, she reached for the wineglass he offered her and dipped her head to hide behind the curtain of her hair.

'Don't do that. Not with me.'

She froze, anticipation and vulnerability sending both hot and cold bolts through her simultaneously. He stepped forward and brushed the hair away from her face. His thumb was warm and slightly rough on the skin of her cheek. The tips of his fingers threaded through the hair above her ear until he held her head in his hand. She couldn't help leaning in to it, letting him support her.

Slowly, he tipped her head until she was looking him in the eyes.

'You don't have to hide from me.'

Oh, she would have given anything to believe that was true. Tears sprang to her eyes and clung to her lashes. Even in the bright sunshine, she could see his pupils growing, become darker and darker. But it wasn't just desire she could see there. Deep in the blackness were the answers to all the questions she'd ever wanted to ask.

Yes, the eyes said. Yes, you are good enough. Yes, you deserve to be loved like this.

One tear escaped, pulled by gravity, and raced away down her cheek. She couldn't move, not even to swipe it away. It carried on running as he continued to stare at her, his expression full of texture and depth, until it trailed down her neck.

A question flickered across her face—she felt it as surely as the salty river air.

Do you?

He didn't move a muscle, except to stroke the skin of her temple with the edge of his thumb. The eyes held the answer once again. *Yes.*

Something inside her, something that had been clenched tight and hard for years, unfurled. And Ben Oliver stepped back into the cool darkness of the boathouse, pulling her with him and repeated his answer over and over again with his lips on hers.

Louise woke up with a gasp, her eyes wide. The fire was little more than burnished embers and a talk show host was skilfully plying a reluctant guest with questions on the television.

She pressed a hand to her pounding chest. Just a dream. It had only been a dream. Calm down, you daft woman. Is this how pathetic you've become? A man shows you just a little bit of concern and neighbourly decency and your subconscious decides he's the love of your life? Just how starved of affection have you been?

Well, her subconscious could just think again. Starving or not, this was one meal she was going to refuse. All her brain had done was jumble up the events and people of her day with the events and characters of the late-night film. A simple crossing of wires, that was all. In the morning, when she was coherent again, she'd make sure everything was rerouted back the right way.

She straightened the stiff arm she'd been lying on and was rewarded with a click. Serves you right for falling asleep in front of the telly, she told herself. Although love *should* be like falling in love in a cheesy old movie, it wasn't. And it never would be. The sooner the right side of her brain caught up with that fact, the better.

At three-thirty the following afternoon, Louise still wasn't sure if she'd won the battle with her subconscious. She pressed the doorbell on the Olivers' cottage door and tried to work out where all the butterflies in her stomach had migrated from. Wherever they had come from, it seemed they were making themselves at home.

There was a click and the door started to open. Louise stopped breathing.

The blonde-haired woman who answered frowned slightly. 'Yes?'

Louise swallowed. 'I'm…er…here to help Jasmine. Mr Oliver is expecting me.'

The woman nodded, opened the door wide and Louise stepped inside and followed her into a funky modern kitchen with glossy red cabinets and black granite work surfaces. Not exactly what she'd pictured Ben Oliver would have chosen but, then again, maybe he hadn't chosen it. Maybe Mrs Oliver had had something to do with it.

Right there was a good reason to stamp on all the butterflies waltzing inside her. Both she and Ben had too much history, too much baggage.

'Hey!' Jasmine was sitting on a cushioned stool next to a breakfast bar with a glass counter. She jumped off and walked towards Louise, her hands in her pockets. A blush stained her cheeks and she looked at the floor as she came closer.

Louise smiled. It didn't seem that long ago that she'd been all awkward gestures and blushes herself. 'Hey, yourself. Ready to bake?'

Jas nodded. 'Is Jack with you?'

Louise shook her head. 'He's gone to football and then to a friend's for tea.'

'More cake for me, then!' Jas giggled.

'Is…um…' Louise glanced at the anonymous woman, who was standing in the doorway, staring at her with undisguised curiosity. 'Is *everyone* joining in?'

'Oh, no.' Jas shook her head. 'Just you and me.' She scowled at the woman, who took the hint and sloped away. 'Don't mind Julie. First of all, her nose is out of joint that she can't stay and snoop on a famous person, but most of all she's probably worried she won't get as much child-minding money if you're looking after me.'

'Your dad's not here?'

'Nah. He doesn't finish work until five o'clock and probably won't be home until six. She looks after me until then most days.'

Louise wasn't sure whether to be relieved or disappointed. Relieved, she told herself quickly. It was much better to be relieved. Still, that didn't explain the black hole that had opened up inside her tummy that the butterflies were now being sucked into.

Even before Ben's key had turned in the lock the most amazing smells hit his nostrils: warm butter and cinnamon, sugar and vanilla. He'd been on a site visit most of the day and lunch had merely been a fleeting fantasy as he'd tried to explain to his client, in the most polite way possible, that his ideas for a visionary garden were actually going to be a blot on the landscape. His stomach rumbled, and he ordered it to get a grip.

He didn't want any cake. He didn't want to be hungry for anything at all.

He found Julie sulking in the sitting room reading a magazine. She really wasn't the greatest substitute for the regular childminder, but at least she'd been amenable to relocating to the cottage today so Jas could cook. With Louise.

His stomach gave up growling and did something more akin to a backflip.

Get a grip, Ben.

It meant nothing. It would always mean nothing. He'd just not been on a date for a while, that was all. He nodded to himself as he made his way to the kitchen. That was it, he was sure. Lack of female company had left him a little hypersensitive to having a woman around. Especially a woman as beautiful as Louise Thornton. It was just his testosterone talking.

But did it have to yell quite so loudly?

His hand was almost on the kitchen door, but he snatched it back and veered off in the direction of his study. He closed the door firmly behind him and let out a long breath. Work would distract him. And he needed to update his files on today's project and come up with something that fulfilled his client's brief to be 'ground-breaking' and 'organic' without being hideously ugly.

Instead of turning his computer on, he reached for a large sketch-pad and a soft pencil. All his best ideas came when he did the designing the old-fashioned way. Somehow, just holding a pencil and having a creamy sheet of cartridge paper beneath it made him want to fill it with shapes and shading and curves, to change the blankness of the bare paper into something that came alive.

He threw the pencil and pad down on his desk, took off his jacket and hung it over the back of his chair, then sat down and set to work, his empty tummy momentarily forgotten.

Half an hour later, he stood back and surveyed his handiwork.

Great, just great. Best ideas? What a laugh.

He squinted at the drawing and then turned the pad ninety degrees. A long, low groan escaped from his mouth and he ran his hands over his face. From this angle, the aerial view of the garden looked like a giant cupcake with a cherry on top. Why, when he'd been thinking of paths and borders, had he come up with this?

Best thing to do was admit defeat. He should just go into the kitchen, say hello and then leave again, proving to himself that he was just working himself up about nothing. And maybe this evening he would call his pal Luke and get him to set him up with one of his wife's friends. Gaby had been trying to matchmake for more than a year now. Perhaps he should just put her out of her misery?

Ben grinned, but it turned into a grimace. The truth was, he didn't really want to go out on a date with anyone. No one he'd met in the last couple of years had been anything more than pleasant company for an evening. No one had been the sort of woman he could envisage fitting into his and Jas's lives. Even Camilla.

Camilla had been stylish and intelligent and funny, but there'd just been no spark—even though he'd done his utmost to get something to ignite. For a while now, he'd just thought it would be better to wait until Jas was older. She deserved love and stability after all she'd been subjected to because of his and Megan's mistakes, not a string of unsuitable girlfriends being tramped through the house. Not that he'd actually brought any of them home, anyway.

Unsuitable. That was a good word.

Louise Thornton was totally unsuitable, no matter how mouth-watering her cakes might be. Okay, she wasn't the airhead the tabloids made her out to be, but her life was full of turmoil, and that was the last thing he and Jas needed at the moment. He'd do well to remember that.

He pushed open the kitchen door and found exactly what he'd feared—turmoil. He blinked at the two females giggling on the other side of the room as a puff of icing sugar billowed up from a glass bowl and settled on them like microscopic snow. 'Not that way…' Louise was saying. 'Gently!'

Jas was laughing so hard she inhaled some of the icing sugar and started to cough and sneeze at the same time. Louise, who was starting to cough herself, patted Jas on the back. Neither of them had any idea he was there.

He looked around the room. On every available space, there were cake tins and wire racks, assorted cake ingredients and almost-clean mixing bowls with finger marks in them. Megan would have had a fit if she'd seen her precious kitchen like this. It looked wonderful.

'Dad!' Jas spotted him, pulled away from Louise and ran over to him.

'Jasmine.' He tried very hard to keep a straight face. Someone had to bring some sanity into the proceedings.

'Come and see what we've made!'

Before he could argue, she slipped a sticky hand into his and pulled him across the kitchen to where a row of cooling racks stood, with various cakes, all in different stages of decoration. Louise was there, standing straight and tall. She'd been laughing a moment ago, but now her eyes were watchful and her mouth was clamped shut. He saw her gaze sweep around the kitchen.

'Sorry,' she mumbled. 'We kind of got carried away.'

He wanted to say something grown-up, sensible, but not one word that fitted the bill entered his head. He was too distracted by the smudge of icing sugar on Louise's nose.

'What?'

'You've got—'

Ben leaned forward, meaning to brush it away, but she stepped back and went cross-eyed trying to see what he was looking at. Then she rubbed at her nose with the heel of her hand, which only served to add a drop of jam to the proceedings.

He stayed where he was. She could sort herself out. It was better that way.

Louise was staring at him. Slowly, she walked over to the double oven and checked her reflection in the glass door. He handed her a piece of kitchen towel and she took it, without looking at him, and dabbed at her face. When she stood up again, she was blushing.

It was so unlike her normal armour-plated façade that he couldn't help but smile. 'Much better.'

She blushed harder and smiled back. 'Good,' she said quietly.

Only he wasn't sure if it was better. There was something rather appealing about an icing sugar covered, vanilla-smelling Louise Thornton in his kitchen. She seemed…real. Not unapproachably beautiful or spikily vulnerable. Just real.

'It's time we started clearing up, Jas.' Louise reached for a tin and headed for the dishwasher.

Ben waited for the whining to start, but Jas just nodded and started closing up bags of flour and putting egg cartons back into the fridge. He shook his head, then decided to put the kettle on—mainly to distract himself from the rows of cupcakes, sitting silently on the counter, just *waiting* for someone to notice them. Saliva started to collect in his mouth and he found himself swallowing three times in a row.

He turned round to offer Louise a cup of tea and found her standing right behind him, a plate full of cakes in her hand. He swallowed once again.

'Would you like one?'

Now, if it had been Jas doing the offering, he would have immediately responded with, *What do you want?* However, Jas was earning her halo washing up the wooden spoons. He looked at Louise and just nodded.

'Raspberry and lemon muffins, jam doughnut muffins or iced fairy cakes?'

His eye fell on something golden-yellow and covered in sugar.

She smiled. 'Jam doughnut muffin it is, then.' She looked down at the cakes for a few seconds, then up into his face. 'Actually, I'm trying to butter you up.'

She was? 'You are?'

Louise nodded. 'I saw something on the television last night…' her eyes glazed over and she seemed adrift for a few seconds before she caught herself and carried on '…about Laura Hastings and Whitehaven. The garden…well, it looked lovely and I wondered if you'd consider…um…taking on the job of restoring it for me.'

He was speechless. For years he'd wanted to have free rein at Whitehaven. Now was his chance. He should be whooping with joy and dancing round the kitchen hugging someone—hugging *Jas*, of course.

'You do that kind of thing, don't you?' She was looking at him strangely.

Twice his head dipped in a nod. He'd started off in landscape gardening and when that had been going well, he'd trained as a landscape architect. The resulting design practice, with special-ist teams to do the ground work when required, was one of the things that made his firm so successful. However, he didn't seem to be able to articulate any of this to Louise.

'Good. Perhaps we can chat another day—during work hours. I don't expect you to give up your time to…' A tiny frown creased her forehead and she stared at him for a couple of seconds, then her gaze dropped to the plate in her hands. 'Still want one?'

The muffin was still warm when he picked it up and, when he bit into it, liquid raspberry jam burst out and added its acidity to the dense but moist texture of the muffin. Pure heaven. Louise just nodded. Oh, she knew she was good! She knew exactly how much her baking had reduced him to a salivating wreck. And she was enjoying it.

Ben stood up very straight and resisted the urge to lick the sugar off his fingertips. Suddenly, this wasn't just about cakes any more. Perhaps it had never been about cakes.

Yup, he was pretty sure he was in big trouble. Because, despite all his efforts at logic, he was starting to think that, far from being the wrong kind of woman, Louise Thornton might suit him just fine.

December, so far, had been incredibly mild, but a cold snap was coming. He could feel it in the slicing wind that raced every now and then up and down the river. Ben hunched his shoulders up to try and escape the draught snaking down the back of his neck as he steered the little dinghy through the sharp, steely waves.

Jas moved into the stern with him and he held up an arm for her to snuggle under. He smiled down at her and she buried her head further into his side. His lips were still curved when he returned his attention to the river. It didn't matter if the weather was cold enough to freeze the Dart solid, the fact that he'd managed to create a living thing so wonderful would always melt his heart.

This was one of those perfect snapshot moments that would live in his memory for ever. Everything on the river seemed to be in shades of grey and silver—the waves, the reflection of the pearly sky. And, directly in front of him, perched on the hill like a queen on her throne, was the bright white house he was heading towards. In their waterproof coats—his dark green and Jas's vibrant purple—they were the only blobs of colour on the river spoiling the effect.

'Do you think it's going to snow, Dad?'

He pursed his lips, thinking. 'I don't know. It would be nice, though, wouldn't it? The last time we had a white Christmas I was a boy.' He hugged Jas to him, then released her as they neared the jetty below Louise's boathouse. 'We'll have to wait and see.'

After tying up the dinghy, he stood for a moment and stared up the hill. The house was hidden by the curve of the land and by the trees, but he knew in which direction it was.

There were ugly gashes in the earth near the house which his team had created in the midst of doing the hard landscaping. It would look a mess when he approached the front lawn. But, in his experience, things often had to get a lot messier before they were transformed into something beautiful. In the spring, the digging and paving would be finished and they'd be able to plant. Come summer, Whitehaven's garden would be transformed. And, over the years, it would mature into something unique and stunning.

Unique and stunning…

How easy it was for his thoughts to turn to Louise.

Recently Jas had taken to showing him any photographs of

Louise which she found in the Sunday papers or magazines. Most of them weren't current, as she hadn't really been anywhere to be photographed recently. Photographers who turned up in the village these days were often sent on a wild goose chase by the locals, who had warmed to Louise as quickly as he had and were now very protective of the celebrity in their midst.

'Ready, Jas?'

Jas, who had been throwing stones into the water, nodded and ran off up the hill. Ben tucked his hands into his pockets and strolled after her. As he walked, an image from an article in one of the Sunday magazines filled his head. Tobias Thornton had given an extensive interview about his new life with a blonde actress whose name Ben was struggling to remember. Of course, there had been photos of Louise and Toby in their glory days.

He punched his hands deeper into his pockets. What did it mean if he admitted to himself that the photos had made him feel sick? He couldn't figure out why; they were fairly innocuous shots of the then Mr and Mrs Thornton on the red carpet somewhere. The body language had been convincing—he'd had an arm around her waist and she'd hooked a hand around his neck. They'd been smiling.

Ben kicked a stone on the path and watched it hit a tree trunk, then roll down the hill out of sight. And then he thought about her eyes. There had been a deadness there, just a hint. Most people, if they'd noticed it at all, would have just assumed it was because it had been the five-hundredth photo they'd posed for that evening. Not him.

That same soul-deep weariness had been in her eyes the day he'd first met her, and no one had been watching her then. He had a good mind to track her ex down and give him a piece of his mind for putting it there.

Ben stopped in his tracks. What he really wanted to do was punch Tobias Thornton's lights out. When had he suddenly got so primitive? He never wanted to hit people. It just wasn't him. Not even Megan's new man. Actually, he felt kind of sorry for that guy…

Slowly, he started walking again, then picked up speed because he realised that he couldn't see Jas any more. He called out and a few moments later saw a flash of purple in between the trees up ahead.

His heart rate doubled. Would Louise be up there on the lawn, strolling as Jack played? Or would she be waiting for him in the kitchen, the kettle blowing steam? He could easily have sent a guy to care for the carnivorous plants in the greenhouses, but he'd kept on coming on Sundays, hoping she wouldn't ask him why he still dealt with it personally.

Sunday was now officially his favourite day of the week. And he had a feeling that Louise knew the plants were just an excuse. Each week they spent more and more of his visit talking, walking round the grounds. He'd never drunk so much tea in his life. But if those giant mugs kept him leaning against the rustic kitchen counters while she hummed and pottered round the kitchen, stopping every now and then to smile at him, how could he complain?

At that moment the trees parted and he saw her. It felt as if every molecule of blood had drained from his body. She was chasing both Jack and Jasmine, who were running round in circles, and when she saw him she stopped, brushed the hair from her face and waved.

Normally, he didn't have any problem speaking his mind. He was never rude or insensitive, but he just called things as he saw them. So why, when all he could think about was asking her out to dinner, or see if they could spend some time alone—just the two of them—did the syllables never leave his lips?

He was now within shouting distance. Hands that had been cold and stiff were now clammy in his pockets and he took them out and did a half-wave with one hand. Louise smiled and his insides jumped up and down for joy. The warm laughter in her eyes erased any form of sensible greeting.

Just admit it, Ben. You've got it bad.

* * *

He was here.

She waved, just to seem friendly. And, of course, if she didn't smile it would look funny, so she did. Only she didn't seem to be able to control how wide, how sparkling it was.

He took long strides across the lawn, minding the gouges of red earth revealed by the landscaping team. Something to do with re-establishing the rose garden, she'd been told. The details were a little fuzzy at present. He gave a little wave, but his face remained serious.

She didn't care. She liked it when he looked serious. His jaw would tense sometimes when he was in this kind of mood and his eyes became dark. She allowed herself a little sigh before he got close enough to see the exaggerated rise and fall of her chest.

She was playing with fire, she knew. But there was nothing wrong with fire if you kept your distance, let it warm you but not scorch you. And that was what she intended to do. To keep her distance from Ben Oliver—romantically, at least. But it had been so long since she'd felt this alive.

What was the harm in a little crush? To feel her blood pumping and all those endorphins speeding round her system. It was good for her. And no harm ever came from a little bit of daydreaming.

That was all it would ever be. That was all she would allow herself.

It would be enough, because to indulge in more just wasn't a good idea for her—or Jack. She'd felt this way before—worse, even. She'd fallen so totally in love that she'd lost herself completely, had allowed herself to become completely overshadowed. It would happen again if she let it. She couldn't help herself. When she fell, she fell hard, completely.

She took a sideways look at Ben as he joined her and they silently started walking towards the kitchen. Jas and Jack had already disappeared inside and were probably trying to work out how they could raid the biscuit barrel without being rumbled.

He was walking with his head bowed, looking at the ground

in front of his feet, but he must have sensed her looking at him, because he mirrored her and the smallest of smiles crossed his lips. Without warning, another sigh sneaked up and overtook her.

Ben Oliver represented all she'd ever wanted in a man, she could see that now. He was strong and kind, thoughtful and funny—although sometimes without meaning to be, but that just made it all the more charming.

He was all wrong for her, of course.

Or maybe, more to the point, she was all wrong for him. She could picture a new wife for Ben quite clearly in her mind: someone who was capable and strong. A woman who had a quiet confidence, a gentle heart. And when evening came, and it was time to turn out the light, he would reach across and stroke her face with the palm of his hand, look deep into her eyes…

Tiny pinpricks behind her eyes took her by surprise and she was glad they'd reached the back door and she could busy herself removing her coat and hat and putting the kettle on before she had to face him again.

He hadn't said it out loud, but she knew he would do anything to keep his and Jas's life on an even keel. And so it should be. It was just such a pity that the only thing she could bring him were the ups and downs of a rollercoaster life—a life that was way out of control and she was powerless to stop. She didn't wish it on herself, so how could she wish it on him when he'd worked so hard to build a solid foundation for himself and his daughter?

Louise watched Ben as he sat down with the kids at the kitchen table and refereed as they argued about who had had the most cookies. Another sigh. And this one hurt right down to her toes. If only this could be real…

She shook herself and made the tea. There was no point wishing for things that couldn't be, but something about Ben made her feel whole, alive in a way she'd never known. So she was going to hang on to that feeling as long as she could and use this crush, this infatuation—whatever it was—to help her heal.

And, one day, when she was good as new, she wouldn't need to dream about him any more and she'd let the fantasies go and watch them swirl up into the air and blow away like the autumn leaves.

If offer card is missing, write to Harlequin Reader Service, 3010 Walden Ave., P.O. Box 1867, Buffalo, NY 14240-1867

NO POSTAGE
NECESSARY
IF MAILED
IN THE
UNITED STATES

BUSINESS REPLY MAIL
FIRST-CLASS MAIL   PERMIT NO. 717   BUFFALO, NY

POSTAGE WILL BE PAID BY ADDRESSEE

Harlequin Reader Service
3010 WALDEN AVENUE
PO BOX 1867
BUFFALO NY 14240-9952

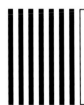

CHAPTER SEVEN

LOUISE had convinced Jack to help her make gingerbread decorations for the Christmas tree. However, she'd overestimated the attention span of an eight-year-old less than a week before Christmas. Once Jack had consumed vast amounts of biscuit dough—mainly while she'd been demonstrating how to use the different shaped cookie cutters—he'd run off. She'd had to tell him off for sliding down the banisters twice already.

Carefully, she removed another tray of golden-brown angels from the oven, replaced them with uncooked stars and shut the oven door. They'd have enough biscuits for ten Christmas trees once they'd finished.

Later this afternoon, once Jack calmed down a little, they'd decorate the tree in the drawing room. She couldn't wait to see his little face when they dimmed the house lights and hit the switch for the twinkling lights. Yes, late afternoon would be best, when the sun was behind the hills and everything was getting gloomy.

In the meantime, she had twelve minutes to kill until the next batch of biscuits was ready. As she scooped the slightly cooled angels off the baking sheet and on to a cooling rack she drifted into one of her top ten daydreams…

It was a balmy summer day. A large picnic blanket was stretched out in the walled garden. Somewhere in the distance children squealed. Her eyes were closed and her head lay on

Ben's lap as he twisted lengths of her hair around his finger, then released them again. Time had slowed, the seconds now hummed out by the bees in the lavender rather than the hands of a clock.

Louise sank into a chair and rested her elbows on the kitchen table. Supporting her chin in her hands, she shut out reality by lowering her lids.

In the daydream, she opened her eyes. He was looking down at her, pure admiration on his face, and she knew he saw into every part of her. It took her breath away. For so long, all she'd seen in men's eyes was a certain wolfish hunger. They admired the packaging, but very few were prepared to take the trouble to unwrap it. And those who did, like Toby, considered the gift inside disposable.

She shook her head. This was supposed to be the bit where Ben leaned in to kiss her, and she was not having it invaded by the likes of Toby. He had no place here in her summer garden.

Just as the imaginary Ben blocked out the sun by leaning forward, leaving her in a cool shadow, better able to see his darkening pupils… Just as she could feel his breath on her skin…

The phone rang. The real phone.

Damn!

Louise snapped her eyes open and she jumped up from the chair. She could let the answering machine get it, but whoever it was would only ring back and interrupt her later. Reluctantly, she grabbed the handset from its cradle on the kitchen counter.

'Hello?'

'Hello, Louise.'

The rich, deep voice was as familiar to her as her own. All thoughts of bees, lavender and sunshine washed from her head on a tidal wave of irritation. 'Toby.'

She wasn't going to ask him how he was; she was past caring, actually. And she certainly didn't need to hear about his cosy new life with twenty-three-year-old Miranda, thank you very much.

Toby said nothing, and she was tempted to put the phone down on him. He'd always done this—made her do the talking, ask the questions, prise information out of him. Well, she wasn't playing his games any more. He obviously had something to tell her or he wouldn't be phoning. He could just spit it out all on his own.

He coughed. Nope, she still wasn't biting. Not even to say, *What do you want?* This time *he* could do all the work, do all the giving instead of the taking.

'Louise?… I wanted to talk to you about Christmas.'

'Talk away.' She leaned against the counter and waited.

'Well, you see… I've been given a freebie, a holiday in Lapland. And I wondered if you'd mind if Jack came with me.'

Louise's stomach went cold. She'd been trying very hard not to think about the fact that Jack was spending Christmas Day and the following week with his father. It would be her first Christmas without him. But Lapland… Jack would be enthralled!

'That's fine with me, Toby. I'll pack warm clothes for him. Are you still coming down on the twenty-fourth to pick him up?'

There was an uncomfortable silence for a few seconds.

'Toby?'

'The flights are booked for the twenty-second.'

Monday? That was a whole three days early! Just like that, the bottom fell out of Louise's Christmas.

'Can't you change it?' she asked, forgetting to hide the panic in her voice.

'Sorry. It's now or never.'

'I… I…'

Toby let out an irritated breath. 'Come on, Louise. Lapland. Jack will love it—and I've missed seeing him for the last month because I've been on location. It will be just Jack and me. Father and son time. He needs it.'

Unfortunately, Toby was right. Jack did need it. He'd missed his dad terribly since he'd left Gloucestershire.

'Just you and Jack? What about…' she wanted to say *her*, but she managed to force her mouth into the right shape '…Miranda?'

There was a sigh on the other end of the line. 'Miranda is… Actually, Miranda's history.'

Her eyebrows rose. Really?

'I miss you, Lulu.' His voice had that soft, gravelly tone that used to turn her insides to mush.

'I'm sorry, but you'll just have to get over it, Toby.'

She shuddered. No way could she ever go back to that life. No matter how far the tabloids thought she'd fallen, or how many celebrity magazines had her at the brink of suicide. She knew in her heart that she was free, happier now than she'd been in more than twenty years.

'Don't be like that, hon. I'm just trying to be friendly.'

It all came sharply into focus. Poor little Miranda probably hadn't realised what hard work a movie star fifteen years her senior would be. And Toby was a movie star who'd grown used to having absolutely everything his own way for most of that time.

Guilt washed over her. That was partly her fault. She'd let him get away with murder, had fooled herself she'd been doing it out of love, when really she'd just been scared he'd see through her glamorous exterior and reject her if she wasn't everything he wanted.

Well, he had. And she'd survived.

No way was Mr Tobias Thornton talking her into being his doormat again! She pulled the phone away from her ear and stared at it, desperate to tell him to go to hell. However, she had to keep the relationship amicable for Jack's sake. It was hard enough for a kid to have to deal with his parents' divorce, let alone hearing the bullet points of every argument in the playground. This wasn't about her; it was about Jack.

'Okay. You can take Jack to Lapland, but I want extra time at Easter.'

Toby blew out a breath. 'Thanks. I'll need to pick him up tomorrow afternoon. We have to leave early Monday morning from Gatwick.'

Disappointment speared through her, harder and deeper than before. 'Fine. See you then.'

She hung up without waiting for any pleasantries and drew in a long steadying breath. Now all she had to do was tell Jack the good news without bursting into tears.

There was a strange car parked slap-bang in front of Whitehaven. Ben noticed it the moment he stepped out of the woods and on to the front lawn. Strange, because it was unknown to him and strange because no one in their right mind would drive such a low-slung sports car in countryside like this. If it rained hard, he'd give the owner five minutes before it stalled in a ford or got stuck in some mud.

He was just wondering if he should check whether Louise was okay when she emerged from the house with Jack in her arms. She was hugging him tight, oblivious to anyone else. A man followed her out of the house, dressed all in black and wearing sunglasses. Ben snorted to himself. They were only days away from the solstice, the shortest day, and there was no crisp afternoon sun, just relentless grey clouds.

The guy removed his glasses and shoved them in a pocket and Ben suddenly recognised him. Weren't most people in films supposed to be shorter and uglier than they looked on screen? Unfortunately, Tobias Thornton was neither. He looked every inch the action hero. He smiled at his ex-wife and kissed her on the cheek. Ben thought he lingered a little too long, but Louise smiled brightly up at him.

Right. There was no use standing here like a lemon. This was family stuff. Private stuff. He might as well go and check on the greenhouses, as he did first every Sunday afternoon.

On reflection, he thought he might have over-pruned the first plant that received his attention in the greenhouse. Seeing Louise and Toby standing there in front of the house had reminded him of all those photos Jas kept shoving under his nose.

It was as if, until that moment, he'd *known* that Louise was Louise Thornton, but the woman in the magazines and the single mother who liked baking had seemed like two very different people. And, suddenly, those two completely separate universes had collided. It had left him reeling. Get a grip, Ben. Time to wake up and smell the coffee.

He spent as long as he could watering and feeding the plants. Then he tidied up the greenhouses and swept the floors. All the while a snapshot of Louise smiling stayed in his head, her lips stretched wide, her teeth showing. He stopped sweeping and rested the broom against the wall.

Suddenly it hit him. That was as far as the smile had gone. Her eyes had had the same hollow look he'd seen in those magazine pictures. She'd been faking it. For Jack.

Ben smiled to himself. The sun was starting to dip low in the sky and he was definitely ready for one of Louise's bottomless cups of tea.

When he reached the kitchen door it was locked. There was no warm cloud of baking smells wafting through the cracks. No light, no noise—nothing. He tried the front of the house but it was the same story. There was no movement in the study or the library. The curved French windows round the side of the house revealed nothing but a darkened drawing room with a bare Christmas tree standing in the corner.

Where was Louise?

Had she gone off somewhere with *him*? Well, if she had, it was none of his business. And, since his work was done here, he might as well go home. Megan was due to drop Jas off in an hour and a half.

He hardly noticed the scenery as he tramped through the woods on the way down to the boathouse. He did, however, spot the loose brick in the boathouse wall as he passed it. Someone might guess the key's hiding place if it was left like that. Slowly, he slid it back into position until everything on the surface looked normal again.

It was only when he had jumped into the dinghy and was about to untie it that he noticed a glow in the arched windows of the boathouse. Someone was in there. And he had a pretty good idea who. What puzzled him was the *why*. Why was she hiding out in a dusty old boathouse when she had a twenty-five-roomed Georgian house standing on the top of the hill?

There was only one way to find out.

He clambered out of the boat again and ran round the back of the structure, up the stone staircase and rapped lightly on the door. 'Louise?'

The silence that followed was so long and so perfect that he started to think he must have got it wrong. Maybe a light had been left on a few days ago…but he hadn't noticed it when he'd arrived. His fingers made contact with the door handle.

A weary voice came from beyond the door. 'Go away.'

A grim smile pressed his lips together. No, his first instinct had been right. She was hiding out.

He pressed down on the handle and pushed the old door open. Everything was still inside. She didn't move, not even to look at him, and at first he was too distracted by the transformation of the once dingy little room to work out where she was sitting. The inside of the boathouse now looked like the inside of a New England cabin. When had all this happened?

The cracking varnish on the tongue and groove walls was gone, sanded back and covered in off-white paint. The fireplace was still there, along with the desk and cane furniture, but something had happened to them too—everything was clean and cosy-looking. Checked fabric in blue and white covered the chair cushions and a paraffin lantern stood on the desk, adding to the glow from the fire.

A movement caught his eye and he twisted his head to find Louise, sitting cross-legged on something that looked like a cross between an old iron bedstead and a sofa, staring into the fire. She turned to look at him, her face pale and heavy. She didn't need to speak. Every molecule of her body was repeating her earlier request.

Go away.

He wasn't normally the kind of guy to barge in where he wasn't invited but, instead of turning around and walking out of the door, he walked over to the opposite end of the sofa thing and sat down, hoping his trousers weren't going to leave mud on the patchwork quilt that covered it.

'What's up?'

Louise returned to staring into the orange flames writhing in the grate. 'Christmas is cancelled,' she said flatly.

He shifted so he was a little more comfortable, avoiding the multitude of different-sized cushions that were scattered everywhere. His gaze too was drawn to the fire. 'That explains the tree, then.'

Louise made a noise that could roughly be interpreted as a question, so he pressed on.

'The one in your drawing room—standing there naked as the day it was born.'

Another noise, one that sounded suspiciously as if she didn't want to find that funny. 'There didn't seem to be much point in decorating it now. Jack's gone to Lapland.'

'Lapland?'

She turned those burning eyes on him. 'Father Christmas? Reindeer? Who can compete with that?'

He shrugged. 'Think yourself lucky. At least Lapland is worth being deserted for. All I'm competing with is a few days in the Cotswolds with Mum and the suave new boyfriend.'

Okay, that got a proper snuffling sound that could almost be interpreted as a chuckle.

'You win, Ben. Your Christmas stinks more than mine. Pull up a chair and join the pity party.' She gave him a long look, taking in his relaxed position on the opposite end of the sofa-bed thingy. 'Not one to stand on ceremony, are you?'

He grinned at her. 'Nope. So…how does one throw a pity party at Christmas? Is it the same as an ordinary pity party or is there extra tinsel?'

A loud and unexpected laugh burst from Louise. Very soon there were tears in her eyes. She wiped them away with the side of one hand. 'You rat, Ben Oliver! You've just ruined the only social event on my calendar for the next two weeks. I'm going to have to reschedule… Will the twenty-fifth suit you?'

It was good to see her smile. He knew from experience just how lonely a childless Christmas could be—and the first one was always the killer.

'This place looks nice,' he said, standing up and walking around the room to inspect it further.

Louise nodded, pulling her knees into her chest and tucking the cream, red and blue quilt over her legs. 'It's not bad, is it? I've even had the windows draught-proofed.' She glanced around the room and then her eyes became glassy. 'I'm tempted just to camp out here for the rest of the festive season. The house is just so…it's too…you know.'

He nodded. The bare Christmas tree had said it all.

He took a deep breath and walked over to her, holding out a hand. She frowned at him and pulled the quilt more tightly around herself.

'Come on.' He wiggled his fingers. 'I've got a lamb casserole that will feed about twenty ready to heat up at home. Come for dinner.'

She didn't move. 'Won't Jas mind?'

'Mind? She'll have so many invitations to go to tea after a visit from you that I'll hardly see her until she's twelve. I'll even let you be miserable at my house, if you really want.'

Louise smiled and shook her head. 'No, you wouldn't.'

He stuffed the hand he'd been holding out in his jacket pocket. 'Don't you believe me?'

'To quote a man I know: "Nope". In my experience, people say they want you to be *real*, but only as long as it involves living up to their expectations of you at the same time.' She wrinkled her nose. 'I learned a long time ago that disappointing them costs.'

He held out his hand again. 'Well, I already know how grumpy you can be, so I wouldn't mind at all if you disappointed me on that front.'

Despite herself, she smiled at him, the firelight reflected in her eyes. 'You're not going to give up, are you?' She lifted her arm, placed her long, slim fingers in his and pushed the quilt aside.

They both smiled as they anticipated his response.

'Nope.'

His hand closed around hers, slender and warm, and he pulled her up to stand. Without her shoes, she seemed smaller and he stared down into her face. The fire crackled and the light of the paraffin lamp flickered and danced. He realised that neither of them had taken a breath since he'd taken hold of her hand.

Louise dropped her head, letting her hair fall over her face, and disentangled her fingers from his. 'I think you're my guardian angel, Ben Oliver.'

He liked it when she said his whole name like that. Somehow it made it seem more intimate rather than more formal. She walked over to a hat stand by the door and pulled her coat off it. While she did up her buttons, she risked another look at him. 'You always seem to be there when I need someone to make me think straight.'

He pretended not to be touched as he turned off the lamp and ushered her out of the door. And he tried very hard not to be stupidly pleased at being what Louise Thornton needed.

Louise locked the door and hid the key in its usual hole and they walked the short distance down to the jetty in silence. He was still mulling it over, standing in the boat with the rope in his hand, ready to cast off, when Louise stepped into the boat beside him and, as she brushed past him to sit down in the stern, she stopped. He felt her breath warm on his face as she leaned close, just for a second or so, and the soft skin of her lips met his cheek.

He whipped his head round to look at her, but she was already sitting on the low wooden bench looking up at him. 'Thank you, Ben.'

A realisation hit him with as much force as the cold waves buffeting the little boat. He *wanted* to be what she needed. And he wanted to *keep* being what she needed. The only thing was, he had no idea if it was a role he could ever play. She didn't need a man in her life right now. What she really needed was a friend. He fired up the motor and untied the boat before heading off across the choppy water.

A friend. Now, that was a role he could manage.

The house seemed empty without Jack in it. Maybe moving to the country had been a mistake. If she'd been staying in London, she could have lost herself in the last-minute Christmas Eve panic in Oxford Street. It might have even been fun to try and spot the most harried male shopper with a look of desperation in his eyes.

Louise stopped by a shallow pool surrounded by bamboo. A copper statue of a Chinese Buddha, covered in verdigris, stared back at her. He was the closest thing to a human being she'd seen since Sunday evening. The statue stared past her, looking serenely through the trees to the river below, and she decided he probably wasn't the life and soul of the party, anyway, and moved on.

She only entered the house to collect a few things and make a flask of tea. In the last few days she'd spent a lot of time at the boathouse, preferring the cosy little space to the multitude of echoes that seemed to have appeared around Whitehaven.

Tonight, she was going to sleep in the boathouse, tucked up under both the duvet and the quilt, with the fire and a good book for company. Hopefully, Santa wouldn't discover her hiding place, set between the beach and the woods, and he'd fly straight past.

She pottered around the house, wandering from the kitchen to her bedroom and back again, picking up the few things she'd need. All the while, she distracted herself with her favourite Christmas daydream. At least in her imagination she could keep the loneliness at bay.

The fire was glowing and coloured fairy lights twinkled on a huge blue spruce in the bay window of a cosy cottage sitting room. It was early in the morning, the sky a deep indigo, and Jas and Jack were fighting good-naturedly about who was going to hand out the presents. She and Ben were laughing and eventually they let the kids get on with it, just to keep them quiet.

Then, amidst the sounds of giggling children and wrapping paper being ripped, Ben drew her to one side and presented her with a silver box with a delicate ribbon of white velvet tied round it. She stopped and smiled at him, a look that said 'you shouldn't have' glowing in her eyes.

Then she gave in and tugged the wrappings free with as much abandon as the children had. Before she opened the box, she bit her lip and looked at him again. Then she prised open the lid to reveal...

This was the bit where she always got stuck. What could be in the box? She didn't want fancy jewellery and body lotion and stuff for the bath was just a bit too *blah*.

Louise stood from where she was, putting a change of warm clothes into a holdall, and stared in her bedroom mirror. You're losing it, girl. Seriously. Hasn't this fantasising about the gardener gone just a little bit too far?

It had. She knew it had. But it was warm and comforting—like hot chocolate for the soul—and heaven knew she needed a bit of comfort these days. She gave herself a cheeky smile in the mirror. *And it's one hundred per cent calorie-free too!*

Her reflection gave her a look that said, *Yeah, right.* She turned her back on it, zipped up the holdall and slung it over her shoulder. The clock on the mantelpiece showed it was three o'clock. She needed to get a move on. No way was she trudging along the rough paths coated with soggy leaves in the dark.

Louise took her time wandering back to the boathouse. There was something hauntingly beautiful about her wild garden in winter. However, when she was only minutes away from her destination, it began to rain—hard, stinging drops with a hint of ice—and she decided to hurry.

She ran up the stairs to the upper level of the boathouse, only pausing to retrieve the key from its hiding place, and burst into her cosy upper room, only to stop in her tracks, leaving the door wide open and a malicious draught rushing in behind her.

What...?

She couldn't quite believe her eyes. What had happened to her sanctuary while she'd been gone?

On almost every available surface there were candles—big, thick, tall ones, the sort you'd find in churches—some balanced on saucers from the old china picnic set she'd rescued from the damp. The fire was burning bright, crackling with delight at the fresh logs it was hungrily devouring. There was holly and ivy on the mantle and, in the corner, near one of the windows...

Louise laughed out loud. How could this be?

A Christmas tree? Not a huge one, but at least five feet high, bare except for a silver star on top. She walked over to it and spotted a box of decorations sitting on the floor, waiting to be hung. Red, purple and silver shiny baubles would look amazing in the candlelight. She picked one out of the box and fingered it gently.

How...? Who...?

An outboard motor sputtered to life outside and suddenly all her questions were answered. She ran out on to the balcony and leaned over. 'Ben!'

The little wooden dinghy was already moving away from the jetty and he looked up at her, a sheepish smile on his face. He waved and yelled something back, but his words were snatched away by the billowing wind.

Her natural response would have been to stand there and shake her head in disbelief, but the rain—which was rapidly solidifying into sleet—was bombarding her top to toe. She pushed her wet hair out of her face, ran back inside and closed all the doors.

Not knowing what else to do, she sat cross-legged in front of the fire, staring at the patterns on the blue and white tile inserts until they danced in front of her eyes. Was this guy for real? No one had ever gone out of their way to do something so special for her before. Her father would have if he'd been able to, but he'd always been so fragile, and it had been her job to look after the others, to cheer them up and keep them strong when things had got tough.

Toby had been good with show-stopping gifts—diamonds, cars, even a holiday villa in Majorca once—but none of those things measured up to this.

Louise stood up and placed a hand over her mouth.

Oh, this was dangerous. All at once, she saw the folly of her whole 'daydreaming is safe' plan. It was backfiring spectacularly. Her mind now revolved around Ben Oliver, her thoughts constantly drifting towards him at odd moments throughout the day. And now her brain was stuck in the habit, it was starting to clamour for more—more than just fantasies. Especially when he did things like this. She was aching for all the *moments* she'd rehearsed in her head to become real.

Heaven help her.

So much for standing on her own two feet and never letting a man overshadow her again. Ben Oliver was an addictive substance and she was hooked. And the last thing she wanted was to lose herself again, not when she'd come so far. In the last few months she'd started to feel less like Toby's wife and more like someone else. It would be so easy to fall into the role of the woman who adored Ben Oliver, and nothing else.

Dangerous.

She looked around the room. As a declaration of independence, she ought to just pack it all up and leave it outside the door, but she couldn't bring herself to do that. If she did, the boathouse would seem as stripped and hollow as the mansion sitting on the hill, and she'd come here to escape that.

The decorations piled in the cardboard box twinkled, begging her to let them fulfil their purpose, and she obliged them, hanging each one with care from the soft pine needles, hoping that the repetitive action would lull her into a trance.

When she'd finished, she pulled the patchwork quilt off the day-bed, draped it around her shoulders and sat on the floor in front of the fire, her back supported by one of the wicker chairs. In the silence, all she could hear was the sound of her own breathing and the happy licking of the flames. She hadn't been sitting there more than a few minutes when there was a knock at the door.

She stared at it.

Whoever it was—and let's face it, she'd win no prizes for guessing who—knocked again. Slowly, Louise rose to her feet, keeping the quilt wrapped tightly around her, and walked over to open it. Her heart jumped as if it were on a trampoline when she saw him standing there, his wet hair plastered to his face, a large brown paper bag in one hand and a rucksack in the other.

'Ben.'

Nice, she thought. Eloquent.

'Louise.'

At least they both seemed to be afflicted by the same disease. He brandished the paper bag. 'Can I come in?'

She stepped back to let him pass and he handed her the paper bag, which was warm and smelled of exotic spices. He moved past her and placed the rucksack on the floor.

'I ought not to let you in, really. Seeing as you've already indulged in a spot of breaking and entering today.' She kept her voice deliberately flat and emotionless.

He stopped halfway through struggling off his green waxed coat. 'You don't like it? Oh, Louise! I'm so sorry. I was just trying to…'

How could she be cross with this wonderful, sweet man? She grabbed the back of his coat with one hand and tugged at it, smiling. 'You succeeded.'

The relief on his face was palpable. 'Thank goodness for that.

I have food in here and I didn't want to have to sail it back across the river and eat it cold.'

She peered in the top of the brown bag. 'Curry? That's not very traditional.'

Ben took the bag from her and began unpacking its contents on to the low coffee table in the centre of the room. 'Nonsense. I'm sure I read somewhere that Chicken Tikka Masala has now overtaken traditional Sunday roast as the nation's favourite dish.'

Louise reached for the old picnic set and pulled out a couple of plates and some cutlery, grateful she'd given it all a thorough wash yesterday. Pretty soon they were sitting in the wicker chairs, feasting on a selection of different curries, pilau rice and naan breads. She broke a crunchy onion bhaji apart with her fingers and dipped it in some mango chutney before popping it in her mouth.

While she ate her bhaji, she looked at Ben, who was absorbed in his meal. Finally, when he glanced in her direction, he froze.

'What?'

How did she say how much this all meant to her? There just weren't enough words, so she settled for simple and elegant. 'Thank you, Ben.'

The hesitation in his eyes turned to warmth.

'Why did you... I mean...why... all this?'

He put his plate down and looked at her long and hard. 'I reckoned you needed some cheering up. I remember how awful it was my first Christmas without Jas.' He gave a half-grin. 'Put it down to me being a single dad with too much time on his hands. Jas is away, my parents live in Spain now and my sister has gone to visit her in-laws. I can't even rely on work to be my saviour— no one wants any gardening done at this time of year.'

Oh, that just sounded too good to be true. Too nice.

'Yes, but you didn't have to do all *this*.' A horrible nagging thought whispered in the back of her mind: nobody does anything for entirely altruistic reasons. He must want *something*. 'I'm not sleeping with you,' she blurted out.

Oh, Lord! Had she really just said that? Her cheeks flamed and burned.

Ben's grin turned to stone and he stood up and practically threw his naan bread down on the table. 'If that's what you think, I'd better leave.'

Instantly, she was on her feet. 'No! I'm so sorry! I don't know what made me say that. After you've been so kind…' At that moment, she hated herself more than she'd ever done for wearing fake smiles in front of the paparazzi and pretending her life with Toby was a glorious dream.

Ben was pulling his coat on, his back to her. She laid a hand on the still-wet sleeve, tears blurring her vision. 'Please, Ben! It's just…' Oh, hell. Her throat closed up and she couldn't hide the emotion in her voice. 'Nobody ever does something for me without wanting something—without wanting *too much*—back. I'm just not used to this.'

He turned to face her, his expression softening slightly. 'Really? No one?'

She shook her head, too ashamed to speak any more. How did you tell a man like him that nobody had ever thought enough of you to make that kind of effort? She always had to earn people's love—by being the one who gave and gave and gave. Even Toby had only kept around as long as he had because it was good for his image, nothing more. And her younger brothers and sisters had grown up thinking she never needed anything, and they had their own lives now. It was their turn to shine. She couldn't burden them with all her problems.

She turned away from him and sank down into the nearest chair, hiding her face in her hands. 'Oh, God. I'm such a mess.'

Ben wasn't sure what to do. Louise had the ability to make his head swim, to prompt him into doing outrageous things that the sensible side of his brain knew he shouldn't be doing. He looked round at the holly, the candles, the stupid tree. It was all too much.

Then he did a double-take and looked at the tree again. It was dripping with baubles. He'd abandoned the box when he'd seen Louise emerge from the woods, deciding it was best not to be standing there like a prize banana when she walked in. But, while he'd been away getting the curry, she'd decorated the *stupid* tree. Hope flared within him.

Louise was sitting, all curled in on herself, staring at the floor. With startling clarity he realised she was one of those people who didn't know how to accept things. She gave of herself constantly—any fool could see that if they looked hard enough—but she'd forgotten that giving was only half of the equation. Or perhaps she'd never known.

He'd pieced enough together from their chats over the last couple of months to realise that she'd had it tough growing up. She'd always had to be the responsible one, the one who carried everyone else. No wonder she didn't know how to receive what had been freely given. And her life since her childhood hadn't helped. Every good deed came with a web of strings attached.

He pulled his coat off and hung it on the hat stand. Louise turned round and stared at him, her mouth gaping in shock.

She hadn't expected him to stay. Not even after her heartfelt apology. Why did she think so little of herself?

He refused to answer the questions written all over her face with words. Instead, he walked calmly over to the chair he'd just vacated, sat down and crossed one leg over the other, resting his ankle on the other knee. She arranged her features into a more neutral expression and relaxed back into her chair, but her hands stayed tightly clasped in her lap.

'I don't know about you,' he said, 'but I could do with some dessert.'

Louise's mouth formed a circle of surprise. 'Dessert?'

He smiled to himself and reached down into the rucksack he'd dropped by the chair earlier and pulled out a bottle of red wine. Nothing extravagant. Just a bottle of supermarket Cabernet.

In one smooth second, Louise unclenched. She smiled at him,

started to speak and then just shook her head. She rose, extracted a couple of teacups from Laura's picnic set and plonked them on the coffee table. Thankfully, the bottle had a screw cap, because he doubted the picnic set came complete with corkscrew. After pouring a generous amount of wine into each cup, he handed one to her.

'A toast—to Christmas,' he said as they cheerfully clinked teacups.

Louise just laughed. 'Something weird is happening here… To Christmas!'

Ben took a sip of the warm, rich wine and kept his thoughts to himself. He knew exactly why he'd phrased the toast that way. Christmas was about giving—and receiving. That weird feeling Louise didn't recognise? That was the joy of letting someone show you how much they cared. If there was one thing he could give as a present this Christmas, it would be to show her that not all gifts had hidden traps, and that receiving them could be a pleasure.

She needed a friend. A true friend. And that was the sort of gift a *friend* could give safely.

As they worked their way through the bottle of wine, a tiny teacup at a time, they retreated to the sofa thing that was piled high with cushions. Even though it was on the opposite wall to the fire, the boathouse's upper room was small enough for them to get all the benefits of its warmth. They talked about anything and everything before falling into a comfortable silence. The candles flickered, the sun set and the temperature outside began to drop.

He was just starting to think that it was about time to get going when Louise suddenly said, 'I don't think I know who I am any more.'

Uh-oh. Good deeds, practical gestures, he was good at. Touchy-feely, girl-type conversations were not his forte. Thankfully, Louise seemed happy for him just to listen.

'The curse of being an ex-WAG,' she said, turning to smile at him weakly.

What was a WAG, anyway? He'd never been exactly sure what the term meant.

'Short for "Wives And Girlfriends",' she added, obviously able to read the look of confusion on his face. 'Probably more accurately used to describe the other halves of famous sportsmen, but it seems to fit me too. WAGS hunt in packs, love shopping and having their photographs taken and—above all—they love *bling*.'

'You're not a WAG!' he said, rather too quickly, forgetting he didn't know what to say in situations like this.

'Well, not any more—having divorced Toby.'

Ben shook his head, frowning. He couldn't see how that definition could ever have applied to Louise. She hated having her photograph taken! He was about to say so, but she preempted him again.

'Oh, I was at the start,' she said. 'I embraced it wholeheartedly—the parties, the magazine covers, the *bling*.' She chuckled to herself.

Didn't she realise what a rare quality that was—to be able to laugh at oneself?

'But, eventually, it grew old. I was famous because of him, because I was Tobias Thornton's wife, not because of anything I had done.'

He shifted to face her a little more. 'I thought you were a model when you met him.'

She nodded and looked into her teacup of red wine. 'I was. And we made it work at first. But it was hard to keep a marriage going when we spent weeks at a time on different continents. And then Jack came along and it seemed only right to give him a home and some structure…'

Why was she punishing herself for that? That was Louise all over—she'd thought of her family first instead of selfishly pursuing what she wanted.

She was lost in a daydream, staring at the rain lashing against the windows. There was a wistful expression on her face, as if she was remembering something or wishing for something she couldn't have.

Maybe it was time Louise did something for herself, got something for herself. Not out of selfishness, but because she deserved it. He rubbed his chin with his thumb. Now all he had to do was to discover what she wanted.

Pulled out of her daydream by some unknown thought, she turned her head, and the look she gave him sent a shiver up his spine.

Surely not.

Her pupils were large and dark, and there was such a heat in her eyes. He'd received that kind of look before from women, but he'd never expected to receive it from her. Surely, she didn't want... him?

His heart rate tripled.

Uh-oh. That put Being What Louise Needed on a whole new level.

CHAPTER EIGHT

WHAT she really needed, Louise thought, was to stop looking at Ben as if he were a Christmas present she wanted to unwrap. It was easier said than done.

The different-sized baubles on the Christmas tree twinkled, reflecting the light from the candles placed all around the room. This wasn't her festive daydream, starring Ben, but it was close. There was the tree, the fire, the sense that someone had thought about her for a change…

Actually, reality was better. The meal, the wine, the companionship had been a much sweeter present than the anonymous gift in the silver box in her fantasies. But, whatever was missing, whatever had changed from her daydreams, one thing remained the same. Ben. It all revolved around him.

The other thing she needed to do was to stop babbling on about losing herself. But the babbling was helping keep a whole other set of urges at bay, so it would do nicely for now. She folded her hands in her lap and smiled at him. 'So…that's what I am. A WAG. A woman who defined herself by her husband and is now adrift with no direction in her life, no purpose.'

Ben began to disagree, but she was on a roll, so she just kept going. 'I've got plenty of money, so I don't need to work, but I do need to do more than just look after Jack and—' she waved a hand to indicate the freshly refurbished room '—decorate. But, apart from knowing how to pout for the camera, I have no qualifications. I didn't even finish school.'

There. That would scare him off. He'd have to believe she was a bimbo now. Only, when she dared to look at him, he didn't seem convinced. She would just have to try harder.

'Oh, I tried all sorts of jobs while I was married to Toby. He was always encouraging me to do some of the things his friends' wives were up to. I did the whole charity circuit, then I tried a bit of television presenting on a fashion show—and was supremely bad at it.' She let out an empty little laugh and Ben fidgeted on the other end of the day bed. 'They never asked me back. I even designed my own range of sunglasses.'

She looked at Ben and waited for a reaction. He shrugged, as if to say, *So what?*

Yeah, so what? That was what the buying public had thought too. It had been an utter flop.

She took a breath, searching for another stupid exploit to fill the silence with. Nothing came. What a waste. She was thirty-one years old and this was the sum total of what she'd achieved in her life. It was pathetic.

'Why didn't you finish school?'

She looked at Ben, expecting to see that same superior look that many people gave her when they found out that little bit of information. Everyone knew that models were thick, and wasn't she a glowing representative of the stereotype?

'Louise? What happened?'

He genuinely wanted to know. She frowned and looked away. He might just be the first person to ask why.

'Dad's illness got worse when I was about fifteen. Some days he needed me at home. Of course, there were home helps and health visitors, but the area where we lived was poor and the local services were overstretched. On his bad days, it wouldn't have done any good to go to school, because I wouldn't have been able to concentrate anyway.'

Ben reached over and simply took her hand. That one gesture was enough to roughen her voice and moisten her eyes again. She ought to stop, but she couldn't. She'd needed to say all of this for such a long time.

'In my last year of school, when I should have been taking my GCSEs, he deteriorated even further. I'd missed so much by then that I didn't even want to go in. And some of the girls were horrible…you know how girls can be. But Dad was in so much pain, he became angry and difficult sometimes and took his frustration out on me—not physically—just verbally. But I understood, really I did.'

Ben's thumb gently stroked the back of her hand and she felt something hard inside herself crumple. More tears flowed and she pulled her hand away to mop them up with a tissue. Things were getting far too maudlin. It was time to brighten the story up.

'Anyway, Cinderella got her happy ending,' she said brightly. 'Just before my seventeenth birthday I was spotted by a scout from a modelling agency and the rest, as they say, is history.'

He held a box of tissues out to her and she took another one. 'What happened to the rest of your family?'

The noise she made using the tissue was truly disgusting. 'Well, my wages helped buy a new house, pay for university fees and things like that. Sarah, the next eldest after me, is a lawyer now and she emigrated to Australia five years ago. The rest have all gone out to visit her this year, but I didn't want to be away from Jack for that long. Billy and Charlotte still live in London— he manages a restaurant, she's a hairdresser. And Charlie, the youngest, is just finishing university. He wants to be an actor.' She rolled her eyes. 'There's no telling some people.'

Somehow, her hand was back in Ben's and he was stroking it again.

'What about your dad?'

Drat! Why did this man have to be so good at reading between the lines?

'He died less than a year after I started modelling.' She looked into Ben's eyes, desperate in this moment for someone else to understand what she'd done. 'I let him down,' she whispered. 'I should have been there.'

And then she started crying, really crying. None of that sniffing nonsense she'd been doing up until now. Big, fat tears rolled down her cheeks. She tried to talk, but her vocal cords had gone on strike.

Gently, slowly, so she wasn't even sure how they'd got there, a pair of strong arms wrapped around her. Time seemed to slow as she sobbed against his chest, but it could only have been a few minutes.

'I've kind of blown your plan for a Merry Christmas right out of the water, haven't I?' she said, thinking she should pull away but doing nothing about it. 'But thank you for trying. I'm not sure there was ever much hope for a woman who doesn't know who to be any more.'

Ben shifted beneath her. His hands came up to cradle her face and he made her look at him.

No one had ever looked at her that way before, as if she were delicate, precious. Her heart, which had been shrivelled like one of the dates her Auntie June used to serve up on Boxing Day, swelled.

His voice was low and scratchy. 'Louise, you are... I...'

For a man who always knew what to say, he was a little short on words at the moment. That couldn't be a good thing. Ben's features clouded and she could tell he was struggling.

Say something, she shouted in her head. *Tell me! Tell me who you think I am! I need to know!*

He was no longer looking at her, but was staring at a piece of blank wall behind her, his mind whirring and, when he looked back at her, her heart stood still for a beat. In his eyes was a renewed sense of purpose and she knew he had something to say. She waited. And Ben just looked at her as if there weren't adequate words to communicate what he was thinking. Oh, how she wished he would try.

His gaze dropped to her lips and she felt them part slightly and her breath catch.

He was going to kiss her. The world started to somersault.

Slowly, he bent his head to meet hers, giving her ample time to move away if she wanted to. But, despite all her ground rules about keeping things 'safe', about keeping things locked away in her daydreams, Louise found she didn't want to move. She wanted him to come towards her. She wanted to taste him, an experience her daydreams had never been able to provide.

The touch of his mouth on hers was exquisitely tender, soft as a whisper. She closed her eyes and gave up all hope of keeping fantasy and reality separate.

Oh, this was better than she'd ever imagined. As Ben kissed her again, still with the same soul-wrenching gentleness, the nerve-endings in her lips burst into life. He moved his hands from her face, ran them through her hair and pulled her closer to him as he fell back against the pile of cushions.

Louise followed him gladly, relishing the fact that she was in total control. Now, instead of *being* kissed, *she* kissed. Ben liked it—she could tell from the low sound he made in the back of his throat.

They kissed each other sweetly, slowly, as if time had stopped for them and all that existed was this moment. After a while, the intensity of their kisses deepened. His lips sought her neck, her jaw line, her earlobe, and Louise began to tingle all over.

She wanted to lose herself in this feeling. Of being desired. Of being feminine. And of being powerful. It was as if she'd entered a realm where she was who she'd always wanted to be, and she wasn't prepared to relinquish that feeling easily.

Rolling over, she pulled him on top of her, giving her hands access to the strong, broad muscles of his back. Ben responded by running a hand down the side of her torso, skimming the curve of her waist. The air between them crackled and popped like the logs on the fire.

Hadn't she said something tonight along the lines of not

knowing what she wanted? Well, she had no problem pinpointing that now—it was all blazingly clear. She wanted Ben. All of him. Right here. Right now.

Taking a deep breath, she wiggled her hands between their bodies and fiddled with the top button of his shirt. A shiver of nerves ran through her.

There had been nobody else but Toby—and he'd grazed in other pastures. What if she wasn't any good? What if she disappointed him? What if this all didn't live up to the fairy tale in her head? For years, Toby had looked at her with a familiar apathy, and she couldn't bear the thought of seeing the same deadness in Ben's eyes in the morning. She was just going to have to pull out all the stops.

Ben, who had been trailing kisses from her collarbone to just below her ear, went still. Her heart began to pound. Ben looked as if he wanted to stop and say something but just couldn't control himself. He kissed her again—hot and sweet and deep enough to make her toes burn.

She trembled as she tried to find a second button on his shirt, her fingers clumsy in the haze of her desire. Ben dragged his lips from hers and his hand closed over her fingers, which were still fiddling fruitlessly with the button.

'We don't need to rush into this,' he whispered.

She knew what he was trying to do. He was trying to be the perfect gentleman, to give her an out. Her gaze locked with his. 'Perhaps we do.'

Once again, he held her face in his hands and, this time, he delivered the sweetest kiss yet. She wiggled her fingers under his and succeeded in popping the button out of its hole. He gripped her hands more tightly.

'Really, Louise. You don't need someone taking advantage of you when you're feeling vulnerable. Maybe this isn't the right time to make this kind of decision.'

He traced the line of her jaw with his thumb and, although his eyes dropped to look at her mouth once again, he didn't kiss her.

'Why can't I decide what I need?' Even in her own ears her voice didn't sound one hundred per cent convincing. But she didn't want to give up yet. Moments like this were like Christmas itself—fleeting, magical. The day after tomorrow the glitter and the wonder would be gone and life would return to being grey and cold and ever so slightly emptier than before.

A slow, gentle smile crept across Ben's face and she couldn't help but smile back as his eyes glittered with fierce intensity.

'Trust me,' he said. 'We don't need to rush. I'm not going anywhere.'

Louise let out a shaky breath. It was very hard to believe that any of this could survive the night and live beyond the dawn. Her eyes must have betrayed her, because he lowered his head and kissed her again.

Carefully, he shifted until he was lying behind her and she was spooned up against him, her head resting on his arm. He pulled the quilt over the pair of them and they lay in the silence, staring into the fire and drawing strength and warmth from where their bodies made contact.

Louise's eyelids flickered. Her head was filled with crackling fires, spiced wine and silver boxes wrapped with ribbons. She yawned and stretched one arm. That was the best night's sleep she'd had since…

She wasn't alone.

Foggily, she tried to decipher what her senses were telling her. There was a warm body wrapped around her, breathing rhythmically…a strange bed…and a *Christmas tree* in her room?

The Christmas tree!

Her eyelids pinged the rest of the way open and, suddenly, she was very much awake. That warm body tangled with hers belonged to Ben Oliver. She didn't dare move, just in case it was all just another delicious dream.

Slowly, she made herself relax back against him. He

mumbled something in his sleep—nonsense—and hugged her tighter. She smiled.

This was what contentment felt like. She'd forgotten its taste, its flavour.

Her eyes scanned the room once again, this time taking in the details. The fire was out, as were quite a few of the candles, but even with the flickering yellow glow from the few that were left, there was an odd silvery-blue light bathing the room.

Mind you, she'd never been in the boathouse this early in the morning before and she had no idea what time it was. Perhaps this was the colour of dawn down here so close to the river.

No, that wasn't it. Gut instinct told her to go and look out of the window. She dropped one leg over the edge of the day bed and started to move, but Ben grumbled again and pulled her back, nuzzling into the side of her neck.

Half-asleep, he was adorable, but whether he'd feel the same way when he was fully conscious was another matter. She'd humiliated herself last night and the atmosphere between them was bound to be awkward. Things often looked different in the cold light of day. And, thinking about cold light, her curiosity got the better of her and she wriggled out of his arms, wrapping the patchwork quilt around her and leaving him covered with the goose down duvet.

As she stood, and could see out of the window, she gasped. Even a tug at the trailing quilt couldn't stop her running to the door, flinging it wide and walking out on to the balcony.

Snow.

Fresh and white and everywhere. It weighed down the bare branches of the young trees and topped the large stones on the beach so they looked like giant cupcakes. It seemed as if the whole world was buried under a blanket of purity, the past forgotten, everything new.

She twirled around in amazement, taking it all in, then reached for the layer of snow, only an inch deep, that topped the balcony railing. The icy crystals crunched under the weight of her fingertips.

A floorboard creaked behind her and once again she was wrapped up in Ben Oliver. He'd brought the duvet with him and he folded it over them both. She held her breath. She'd thought that maybe he'd been giving her the brush-off last night, but the way he was holding her now, as if he wanted to seal their bodies together, laid those fears to rest. He rested his chin on her shoulder so his head was right next to hers and kissed her cheek near her ear.

'Merry Christmas, Louise.'

She twisted her head to look at him, her eyebrows raised. She'd been so caught up in the magic of last night, the beauty of this morning, that she'd completely forgotten that it was Christmas Day.

'Merry Christmas,' she whispered back, suddenly feeling very shy. But, as she went to shake her fringe in front of her eyes, he stopped her with a gentle hand.

'Don't do that,' he said, moving so they were now facing each other.

She wasn't foolish enough to say, *Do what?* After glancing away for a second, she tilted her chin up and met his gaze.

'That's better.'

He smiled and, just like that, any residual awkwardness she'd been feeling evaporated. There was such warmth and light in his eyes, so many possibilities, that she felt an answering smile spread over her own face. So they stood there like that for goodness knew how long, grinning stupidly at each other, saying nothing and everything.

Then his eyes sobered and began to communicate all sorts of other things. Louise didn't wait for him this time. There wasn't much of a difference in their heights, and she reached up behind his neck and pulled him closer, lifting her heels off the floor just slightly.

Kissing Ben Oliver on a snow-dusted balcony on Christmas morning had to be one of the most romantic things she'd ever done. Not only were the kisses perfect, but the crisp cold air on her cheeks and the chill in her toes only seemed to increase the heat spreading from her core. She felt as if she was glowing from the inside out, so much so that shivers rippled through her.

Ben pulled away, just enough to focus on each other without going cross-eyed, and tucked the quilt tighter around her.

'How do you feel about cold curry for breakfast?'

She grinned. 'My absolute favourite.'

And, as he playfully pulled her back inside the boathouse, she took one last look at the picture-perfect scene outside. The river reflected the colour of the iron sky perfectly and smoke puffed from the chimneys in the village across the river. As far as the eye could see, the rolling hills were bleached and frosted like the icing on a giant Christmas cake.

It didn't matter to Louise if winter had stolen all the shades and tones and left everything monochrome. To her, this morning, life was very much in Technicolor.

Ben ran up to his bedroom, slammed the door open and stripped all his clothes off in under a minute. The last sock still hadn't hit the floor when he'd run into his bathroom and jumped in the shower.

He felt like a man possessed. Like a man with too much adrenaline coursing through his system, who was about to spontaneously combust. Realising he had just started to wash himself with conditioner, he forced himself to stand still and take a few deep breaths.

No good. He still felt like whooping aloud, or running down the street and knocking on every door just to tell them he'd kissed the most astounding, marvellous, complicated woman in the world and, once he was clean and changed, he was going to go back and do it again.

He yelled as shampoo got in his eye.

Slow down!

This time he was more successful. He managed to rest one hand against the tiled shower wall and watch the rise and fall of his chest slow a little. Relax. You can do it.

He finished his shower in a speed that could be classified more as 'brisk efficiency' than 'mania', cleaned his teeth and wandered back into the bedroom, whistling, a towel slung round his hips.

What time was it? He checked the digital alarm clock on his bedside table. Ten.

That meant he'd been gone about forty-five minutes. And it would probably be another hour until he saw her again.

Without really paying attention to what he was rummaging for in his chest of drawers, he pulled out clean clothes and got dressed. One last look in the mirror. He ran his hand through his wet hair, then stilled. Was this what Louise saw? A thirty-six-year old with dark hair and brown eyes? That description could probably fit hundreds of thousands of men up and down the country. Apart from the insane grin he just couldn't wipe away completely, he was just an ordinary guy.

Okay, he wasn't desperately bad-looking, but he'd be kidding himself if he thought he could compete with the men in Louise's world. A world in which he clearly didn't belong.

But Louise isn't with one of them, a little voice whispered gleefully in his ear. *She's with you. She kissed you. Heck, she even wanted to make love with you.*

At that point he told his male pride to get a grip.

Even so, the unquenchable grin widened.

He grabbed his watch, fastened it on his wrist and jumped down the stairs only two at a time. But when he got downstairs he couldn't find his keys. He never lost his keys. He searched the pockets of his jacket, which he found on the floor rather than on its usual hook. Nothing. Rather than dropping it again, he pulled it on.

A panicky feeling started to breathe fire in his stomach. He had to get back! He'd be late!

For what? the sane side of himself said. There's no timetable. So what if you arrive there at five past eleven rather than on the dot?

Okay, now he was scaring himself. He sat down on one of the chairs in the kitchen and thought about where he could have possibly left his keys since he'd run through the front door. Best thing was to retrace his steps. He went to the cottage door, opened it and found his bunch of keys dangling in the lock.

What was happening to him? The sky was under his feet and the earth above his head. When exactly had the universe turned itself inside out so everything was back to front? An image popped into his mind: Louise, wrapped in a quilt, standing on the boathouse balcony, tipping her head up to meet his eyes and daring him to love her.

It was a challenge he hadn't refused, he realised.

He loved Louise.

Now he wasn't so sure he wanted to wake all his neighbours up and share the news. Was he crazy? Quite possibly. How could whatever was happening between them have a future? His head told him to back out now; his heart told him not to lose faith.

With one startling flash he understood that the tables had been turned. He'd set out to be what Louise needed and, in the end, he'd discovered he needed her so badly it hurt. Fear sliced through him at the thought that there might not be a happy ending to this story.

He pulled his keys out of the lock and returned them to his pocket, then closed the door. He'd loved Megan, he was sure of that, but she'd never shaken his foundations like Louise did. What did that mean? Was this romance doomed or did that promise great things?

He ought to stay away, he decided. He ought to make an excuse to back out and stay away. That was the sensible thing to do. He nodded to himself, took off his jacket and carefully placed it on its hook.

Five minutes later he was in his dinghy, motoring across the river in the direction of the boathouse jetty.

* * *

Christmas was its own little universe for Louise and Ben. They shared a festive dinner of lasagne, which Louise found in the freezer, then retreated to the boathouse for the evening, where they talked and laughed and kissed and wished—not out loud, of course. Some things were far too delicate to be spoken aloud.

But this little universe was finite and, as night fell on Boxing Day, ugly reality started to shred the perfect picture they'd created.

Louise was sitting in one of the wicker chairs close to the fire with a book in her lap and Ben was stretched out on the day bed, trying not to doze. Suddenly, he raised his head and looked at her.

'Louise?'

Her heart did a silly leap. Shouldn't she be able to control that by now? It had started on Christmas morning when he'd reappeared, slightly damp and smiling, at her back door with a Christmas pudding big enough for ten and a bottle of port. Now, *that* was the way to spend Christmas. Especially if it involved being spoonfed the pudding in front of the fire.

She couldn't remember a Christmas as perfect. Not even Jack's first Christmas. Toby had spoiled it by getting drunk and disappearing off to a nightclub with one of his useless so-called friends.

'What's up?' she said carefully.

Ben shifted himself on to one elbow. 'What are we doing?'

'Well, I'm supposed to be reading that biography about Laura I borrowed from you and you're trying to pretend you didn't finish off the last quarter of that plum pudding.'

Ben didn't laugh as she expected him to. He gave a half smile, then jumped off the day bed and drew the other chair over so he could sit opposite her. He took her hands in his. 'No, I mean you and me. What is this?'

She folded the book closed and placed it on the coffee table. Laura's carefree smile and laughing eyes in the cover picture mocked her. She bet Laura wouldn't have got all tied up in knots about something like this. Laura would probably have said something droll and had her lover swooning at her feet in this kind of situation. But Ben wasn't her lover, and it seemed that she was the one in most danger of swooning at present. This was all so new—this thing with Ben—that sometimes it felt raw, even though it was wonderful at the same time.

'Ben Oliver, are you asking me if I want to be your girlfriend?'

There. That was as droll as she could manage. But she didn't manage to pull off the knowing sophistication that was supposed to go with it when he leaned in close, gave her a soppy grin and said, 'Yeah, I suppose I am.'

She grabbed him by the shirt collar and pulled him in close for a long, slow kiss.

He rested his forehead against hers. 'It's just that…'

What? Her heart began to thump. It was too perfect. *Something* had to go wrong, didn't it?

'Jas is home tomorrow and…'

She nodded. This had been a time out of time. Tomorrow they had to go back to their real lives, which seemed to be on parallel tracks, running close, but maybe never destined to cross and merge again.

'I understand, Ben.'

He pulled away and looked intently at her face. 'No… No, Louise. I meant…what are we going to say to the kids? Are we going to keep this a secret or are we going to shout it from the rooftops? It's a delicate situation and we need to decide how to handle it.'

Relief flooded through her. Followed hastily by confusion. What *were* they going to tell the children? Jack was the worst blabbermouth known to man. She frowned. 'Do we want to tell *anyone*?'

And, more to the point, what would they say if they did? Everything was so new between them. How should they define it? Of course, there would be far-reaching consequences as well.

'You do realise that we might get media attention if we go public?' she said.

Ben's face was a picture of surprise, as if he'd totally forgotten about that side of her life. That only made her want to kiss him again. Everybody else always saw the glitter first and nothing second.

For the first time in days, she felt as if she were on familiar territory. 'Believe me, you don't want photographers camped on your doorstep. Why do you think I chose to live in such a remote place as Whitehaven? In the village, you and Jas would be easy pickings.'

'Jas?' There was more than a hint of panic in his voice. 'You think they'd take pictures of Jas?'

Just great. This relationship was dead in the water before it had even begun, wasn't it? She knew Ben well enough to know that creating a 'normal' life for his daughter was paramount.

She stroked his arm. 'Who knows? The paparazzi are a law unto themselves. But I think we have to consider the possibility.'

They both stared at one another.

There were no easy answers to this one. The only way to really protect Ben and Jasmine was to call the whole thing off right now. She broke eye contact and stared at her feet. Just the thought of saying goodbye to Ben now made her hurt—physically hurt. Cold fear shot through her. Contemplating the possibility of losing him brought things sharply into focus: somewhere along the line, she'd fallen in love with Ben Oliver.

He gently brushed his fingers under her chin and tipped her face up to look at him. 'Hey.' The word was filled with such tender softness, she felt her eyes moisten. He smiled at her. 'I told you before—I'm not going anywhere, okay?'

She nodded and the cold, sharp feeling gradually withdrew.

'Here is my idea,' he said. 'We tell Jas and Jack—because they're going to work it out pretty soon anyway—but we don't tell anyone else yet. It will buy us some time, give us and the kids a chance to get used to things first.'

Sensible. He wanted to wait before letting the world know, just in case it didn't work out.

'I've got to wait at home for Megan to bring Jas back tomorrow, but I still want to see you.'

Good. She wanted to see him too. And she was greedily going to grab every chance to be with him.

'Jas is due back at noon and it's going to be quiet tomorrow—everyone recovering after Christmas. If you come for one o'clock and drive round, using the lanes rather than coming through the village, nobody will see you. Once you're there, we'll put your car in the garage.'

She smiled at him. Maybe this could be fun. Maybe she'd get to live her dream life for just a little bit longer before it all came crashing down around their ears.

CHAPTER NINE

THE roar of a distant car engine got louder. Ben knew not to hope that this would be Megan bringing Jas back. She'd rung twenty minutes ago saying she was 'running a little late'. And usually when Megan said 'late', she didn't mean ten minutes late. He'd be lucky if he saw Jas before teatime. Megan had probably only just left the country house hotel near Stow-on-the-Wold where they'd been staying—not that her breezy message had communicated anything of the sort. He just knew.

Abruptly, the engine cut out and he dashed outside to open the garage doors. This must be Louise. He checked his watch. Yup, five minutes early. From one extreme to the other.

Mind you, if Louise was an extreme, he was quite happy being stuck out there in left field. Yes, the ride was going to be a little bumpy, but he could really see things working out between them.

Louise grinned at him from her car as he guided her inside and closed the garage door behind her. He walked round to the driver's window and waited as she pressed a button to wind it down. Acting on impulse, he leaned in through the open window and surprised her with a hot, sweet kiss.

The rush of endorphins he got every time he just laid eyes on her was amazing, but a long-lasting relationship took more than just feel-good chemicals whizzing round his system. While Louise wasn't the high-maintenance woman he'd mistaken her for, she was still smarting from a recent divorce. Only a fool would rush in too quickly, and he had never been a fool.

A crick in his neck forced him to draw back and let her out of the car.

'Good morning, yourself,' she said, smiling sweetly at him. Then she looked around. 'Where's Jas? I would have thought you'd have wanted to talk to her first, rather than have her catching us like that.'

He grimaced. 'Megan is running late. So I have you to myself for the next couple of hours. Come on.' He tangled his fingers with hers and pulled her out of the side door of the garage and across the garden, where small patches of snow still lingered. Most of the village was now back to normal, a warm wind from the west having melted the snow in all but the shadiest of spots.

Once through the back door, they fell into each other's arms again. The endorphins started partying.

Louise was different this morning, calmer, more peaceful. Since Christmas Eve she'd been like a skittish horse, jumping at every little thing, sensing danger where there was none. But something had changed. He could tell it from the way she kissed and held him, from the sound of her voice, even the way she moved.

Still kissing her, he pulled her hat and scarf off and threw them in random directions. She laughed against his lips. 'Not fair,' she murmured. 'You've only got your indoor clothes on.'

She undid the top button of her coat, but left the others fastened as she kissed him again. Everything went blurry for a bit and all he was aware of was the sweet spiciness of her perfume, the shallowness of their breathing, the pull of her fingers as they hooked into the belt loops of his jeans and contracted into fists.

Then, after hesitating for a second, she ran her hands under his sweater. He flinched as her cold fingers met his warm flesh, but the sensation was anything but unpleasant. The contrast of temperatures only heightened the sensation. He pulled her closer and deepened the kiss. Louise responded eagerly, surprising him by sliding her hands up his back, taking the sweater with them. Cold air rushed around his torso. Hot blood pumped through his veins.

Finding it impossible to go any further without breaking lip contact, she pulled back from him and continued to tug his top upwards. Just before she pulled it over his head, she looked him in the eyes. They stayed there like that while the kitchen clock loudly announced the seconds.

Wordlessly, he lifted his arms over his head and she disappeared as his sweater blocked his vision. The jumper went the same way as her scarf and hat.

'Not fair,' he said, trying very hard not to let on he was shaking. And he didn't think it was because he was cold. 'You've still got your outdoor clothes on.'

He reached for her, first dealing with the remaining large buttons on the front of her coat and pushing it off her shoulders, before stroking her face with his fingertips. That perfect bone structure might have produced a proud beauty, but he knew that the woman inside was soft and tender, carrying the scars of the years. He wouldn't add to them. He promised himself that.

The teasing humour evaporated and suddenly everything felt very serious, momentous. Should he stop her now? Was she really ready for this? What Louise *wanted* and what Louise *needed* might be two very different things.

'Louise…'

She silenced him with a kiss. 'You have to trust me to make my own decisions, Ben. And I've decided…'

He kissed her fiercely, then drew back to look at her, hoping his eyes conveyed the storm surge of feeling that was crashing over him. 'You know I love you, don't you?' She had to have guessed. It was stamped in every look he gave her, in every touch.

Her lips quivered and she tried to smile. A fat tear rolled down one cheek. 'No, I didn't.' Her answering kiss was rich and soulful. 'But I do now.' Her hands traced the muscles of his chest and he felt them quiver in response. 'Show me, Ben. Show me how much...'

That snapping sound in the back of his head must be his self-control breaking because, right now, he couldn't think about anything but doing exactly what she said. He would. He would show her how much he loved her. He would make sure that she never doubted for a second, ever again, how rare and precious she was.

He kicked her fallen coat out of the way, picked her up and carried her straight out of the kitchen and into the hallway. His foot was on the bottom step when the doorbell rang.

'Cooo-eee!'

Both of them froze.

He knew that irritating little sound anywhere. Megan.

The word he wanted to say, he couldn't, just in case Jas was standing outside and she heard it through the door.

Louise jumped out of his arms and ran back into the kitchen. Megan's blonde head was detectable as she tried to peek through the little window in the centre of the door. Thank goodness the glass was rippled and bowed. The bell sounded again and he jumped.

'Ben? Is that you?'

Realising he couldn't very well answer the door in his present state, he charged back into the kitchen and started to fight with his sweater. Why, in situations like this, did the neck hole and the armholes seem to switch places? When he'd finally popped his head out of the right opening, he ran back to the front door, yelling, 'Just coming!'

Megan did not look impressed when he swung the door open. Jas jumped into his arms. 'Daddy!'

'About time too,' Megan said, pushing past him into the hall. Never mind that she didn't live here any more and, technically, she was supposed to wait to be asked. 'Come along, Jasmine.'

Jas gave him one last kiss and turned to grab the handle on her Sleeping Beauty trolley bag and followed her mother inside.

Ben, in a fit of adrenaline, managed to slam the door, charge past his ex-wife and daughter and make it to the kitchen door first.

Megan eyed him suspiciously. 'What are you up to, Ben?'

He ran a hand through his hair and leaned against the door jamb, blocking her way. 'Nothing.' The problem with priding himself on being a straight-talker was that he didn't get much practice at lying. Megan was looking at him strangely.

'Coffee?' he asked, although the words felt as if they came out sideways. In an effort to maintain harmony and stability, he always offered Megan a drink when she dropped Jas home. Most times his ex was far too busy being fabulous to stop and chew the fat, but today she was showing no inclination to rush off.

'Thanks,' she said dryly and pushed the kitchen door open.

Louise had her hat and scarf on and was just retrieving her coat from the floor and heading for the back door when she heard the door creak open. Quickly, she hung her coat on one of the over-crowded pegs. If she couldn't disappear altogether, she was going to have to make it look as if she'd just arrived. Her skin was still heated and her cheeks were probably flushed. Hopefully, she could blame it on having just come in out of the cold weather.

'Louise!' Jas shot into the room like a bullet and threw her arms around her middle.

'Hey, Jas!' she said softly.

Jasmine looked over her shoulder and shouted at the woman who had just entered with Ben. 'Mum! Look! Louise is here!'

'So she is.'

Ben's ex-wife was nothing like Louise had pictured her. She'd imagined a housewifey sort, but Megan was only what could be described as a 'yummy mummy'. Her long blonde hair fell past her shoulders and ended in a blunt, straight line, and she was wearing a designer coat, military style, pulled in tight at the waist. Her high-heeled boots made a fingernails-on-a-blackboard sort of noise as she crossed the tiled floor and offered her hand.

Louise's jeans, jumper and clumpy fur-lined suede boots suddenly seemed rather casual. She pulled the hem of her jumper down, rumpled as it had been from being whisked into Ben's arms. She'd never thought of Ben as being a man who 'whisked'—the revelation was still doing odd things to her insides.

'Hello.' Not exactly original, but it was polite and it didn't give too much away. Jas, still hyperactive after a longish car journey, abruptly let go of her and dashed towards the door. 'Dad! Wait till you see the really cool presents I got from Nanna and Pops! Can I get them from the boot, Mum?'

Megan nodded and threw Jasmine a bunch of car keys that she pulled out of her pocket. Her exit left the adults in an uncomfortable silence.

'As Jas has already pointed out, I'm Louise. Nice to meet you.'

'Megan.'

Something about this woman reminded Louise of a cat arching with all its fur frizzed up. She noticed that Megan didn't bother removing her gloves to shake hands. Somehow, that made the whole situation easier. Being Toby's wife had made her used to this kind of response from other women. She was always a threat, the enemy, never someone that they wanted to gossip over cappuccinos with.

'I'm doing Louise's garden for her.'

Both she and Megan turned to look sharply at Ben, who seemed to be pulling every mug he could find out of the cupboard.

Garden? Good one. She'd forgotten all about the garden.

'Yes,' she said, nodding a little too hard. 'Ben is sorting out my rebellious garden for me… We were going to have a look at the plans.'

Don't wince, she told herself. You *were* going to look at the plans today—just later. Much later.

'Today? It's still the Christmas holidays.' Megan's voice was flat as she looked at Ben, then at Louise, then back at Ben again. Nobody moved.

Okay, the only way to get round this was to play the rich-and-famous card, much as she hated it. 'Yes. I'm sure you understand, Megan. Life can be so hectic, you know, flying all over the place…' The silly little laugh she gave turned her own stomach. She hadn't meant to do it; it must be the nerves. 'Sometimes we just have to squeeze the project meetings in whenever we can.'

'I'm sure it'll be marvellous,' Megan said, and Ben did a double-take and looked in astonishment at his ex-wife. 'Ben really is very talented.'

Louise stifled a smile as Ben gave her a dry look, held up a large, over-sized teacup kind of a mug and shook his head. Megan's back was to him, thank goodness, so she didn't see him reach for the smallest mug of the collection and, after giving Louise a wicked smile, spooned instant coffee into it.

Megan sat down at the kitchen table, her mouth pursed a little too tightly for Louise's liking. 'I must say, you're all Jasmine has talked about while we were away.'

Louise shot a nervous look at Ben, who was now making a cup of coffee with record-breaking speed. 'Well…Ben has brought Jasmine up to Whitehaven a couple of times. My son, Jack, is only a few years younger than her and it made sense for the children to play together while Ben was looking after the garden.'

Megan nodded and twisted to look at Ben as he plonked the mug of coffee in front of her, then dropped into the seat opposite Louise, his expression guarded.

'Well, Louise, I'm sure you'll appreciate that you're not the only one who leads a busy life. Ben and I have some *family* stuff to discuss—' as she said 'family' she laid a hand on Ben's arm '—so, if you wouldn't mind…'

'Dad!' Jasmine burst back through the kitchen door, her arms full of presents. 'Look what I got!'

Much as Louise would have liked to walk over to Ben, slide her arms around his waist and stake her claim, this was neither the time nor the place.

Ben turned to look at Megan, an exasperated expression on his face. 'Meg, I arranged to meet Louise at one o'clock, she shouldn't have to leave.'

The words *especially as you were late* hung in the air.

Louise did an extra knot in her scarf. 'No, it's okay, Ben. Family stuff comes first. I'll call you when I have an opening in my schedule. Goodbye, Jasmine…Megan.'

She collected her coat from near the back door and Ben rose and escorted her out of the kitchen and into the hall. She looked a little puzzled, but followed his lead. As she reached for the door latch, he grabbed hold of her hand. 'Don't go.'

She bit her lip and shook her head.

He turned her hand over, pulled it to his lips and planted a kiss into her palm. 'Actually, you can't go yet—not without giving away that your car is parked in my garage, which will only make Megan more suspicious.'

Okay, that was true, but she could always use the ferry and come back for her car later.

'If you could just…I don't know…take a walk on the beach for half an hour, I'll see what she wants to get off her chest and then I'll call you when the coast's clear. You do have your phone with you, don't you?'

She nodded. This was getting sticky, complicated, just as she'd feared when Ben had only been a daydream. That was the problem with reality. It was so…messy. She ought to take the ferry and leave them alone. But she found herself scrawling her mobile number on a pad by the telephone in the hall.

Ben closed the door behind Louise and then pressed his face against the little window to watch her disjointed shape walk down the garden path. There were some days when he regretted not being able to make his marriage work, but today certainly was not one of them.

Whatever he did for Megan was never enough. It never had been.

When she'd left him, he'd felt empty. Not really because he'd missed her—by then he'd been too exhausted to feel anything but regret on Jas's behalf. No, the emptiness had been more a sense of being bled dry. He was a pretty decent bloke, he thought, and he'd put his heart and soul into his marriage but, in the end, he'd had to accept that his best was not good enough.

Megan had wanted more. She'd been so needy—he could see that now. Blindly, he'd thought he could help her grow, be the foundation that she could build on. But she was the sort of woman who needed constant attention, constant flattering, and he just hadn't been skilled at that.

He still wasn't. He scrubbed his face with his hands and headed back to the kitchen. It was going to take all his energy for the next half hour to be nice and hear what her latest gripe was without telling her to get over herself.

The young woman who had been broken in spirit had not blossomed into the strong and confident mother he'd thought she would. She was still full of all the same insecurities. And what little confidence she'd possessed hadn't grown into self-esteem, but had hardened into self-involvement. She was the world's axis, and heaven help anyone who didn't agree with her.

When he re-entered the kitchen, he was disappointed to discover that her coffee mug was still mostly full. He sat down beside her.

'So…Megan. What's so urgent?'

She gave him a withering look. 'Thank you, Ben. I had a lovely Christmas. How about you?'

'Dad? Look at this journal… It's got an electronic lock and a password. I can keep all my private stuff in here. Mum says it'll help me grow emotionally to keep a diary.'

Ben resisted the urge to growl. 'It's lovely, Jas.'

Placated, his daughter started to flick through the book, full of 'all about me' pages. He steadfastly ignored the page entitled: '*Boys I like…*'

Turning back to Megan, he raised his eyebrows. She glanced at Jasmine, then motioned for him to join her on the other side of the kitchen. Too cloak-and-dagger for him, but it was easier to play along than have a row in front of Jasmine. He hauled himself back out of the chair and followed her, hoping that filling in the diary would command one hundred per cent of Jas's attention.

Megan's idea of 'subtle' was talking in a stage whisper.

'I want Jasmine to come and live with me.'

He shook his head. Nah-hah. No way. They'd decided all of this when Megan had moved out. Jas needed to stay in Lower Hadwell for school, for continuity. It had been Megan's idea to up and move to South Devon's New Age hotspot to 'discover' herself. He didn't like the idea of Jas being influenced by all of that mumbo-jumbo at such a young age. And some of Megan's friends…

Megan's voice rose. 'She's going to be in senior school come September. I think a girl that age needs her mother close by.'

The rustling noises reaching them from the direction of the kitchen table stopped.

He grabbed his ex-wife by the arm and propelled her out of the kitchen. Megan forgot her stage whisper and protested loudly.

'Pity you didn't think she needed a mother when you upped and left us.'

She ran a hand through her long hair. 'I realise what a mistake that was now, and it's time to put it right.'

'Right for whom?'

Not for him, not even for Jasmine. This was all about what Megan wanted, about what was good for Megan.

'Dad?' A nervous shout came from inside the kitchen.

Still fixing Megan with his fiercest stare, he yelled back, 'I'll be right there, Jellybean.'

'Yes, that's right, Ben. Take the easy way out, run away from the main issue.'

Lord, he really wanted to grab this woman by the shoulders and shake her.

'Megan,' he said from between clenched teeth, 'wouldn't it have been more appropriate *not* to have discussed this in front of Jasmine?'

She made a gesture he could only describe as a flounce. 'It should be her decision, you know.'

Give him strength! 'We are not doing this now! Okay? You are going to collect your handbag, say goodbye to your daughter and leave. And I will phone you during the week so we can discuss this properly.'

Megan glared at him. 'Fine.' She stalked into the kitchen, followed his suggestions to the letter—which had to be a first—slamming the front door behind her. She was going to stew on this for days, he just knew it. Which was only going to make the coming negotiations worse, but how could he let Jas overhear? It would have to be handled carefully, properly.

As he headed back into the kitchen, prepared to dole out plenty of cuddles and one-to-one attention, he heard the screech of tyres in the lane.

Well, that ought to put any of her ridiculous ideas that he was still carrying a torch for her to rest. And about time too.

Louise put her phone away. The coast was clear. Although, from the sound of it, it would be better to leave father and daughter to some quality time this evening. Despite Ben's protests, she insisted she was merely returning to collect her car, then she'd be on her way.

She stepped over the low wooden fence that separated the lane from the stony beach and headed back towards Ben's cottage. Only a moment later, she had to flatten herself against the hedge as a flashy four-wheel drive hurtled towards her.

Megan was in the driving seat and she looked as if she'd just sucked a whole pound of lemons. The car slowed slightly as she spotted Louise. At first, Megan's face registered surprise, but when she got closer her face contorted further and she gunned the engine, leaving Louise coughing on exhaust fumes.

* * *

The following day was Sunday. Through a series of text messages, Louise and Ben had decided that he should come to Whitehaven as usual and, after testing the water, they would tell Jasmine they were together.

As Ben motored across the river in the dinghy, he couldn't wipe the smile from his face. Life had a funny way of throwing surprises at you. If someone had told him six months ago that he'd fall in love with one of the glitzy women from the magazine covers, he'd probably have hurt himself by laughing too hard. But, in his eyes, Louise wasn't one of *them*. She wasn't run-of-the-mill, either. She was a unique individual, braver and stronger than she gave herself credit for.

The hike up the hill towards the house seemed to last for ever. It didn't stop Jas complaining that he was going too fast and pulling on his jacket to slow him down. Finally, he caught a glimpse of white masonry between the trees. Jas started running—probably because she had cakes on the brain.

Two seconds later, he sprinted after her.

When he laid eyes on Louise, who had obviously been hovering in the empty kitchen waiting for him, he hadn't counted on how hard it would be to be only feet away but not able to pull her into his arms and kiss her senseless. Not yet, anyway.

It was torture, having to go out to the greenhouse and look at the plants while Louise and Jas made banana muffins together. They'd decided a little 'bonding' time might help before he broke the news. When he returned, he drank his cup of tea so fast he scalded his throat. Did he care?

'Come on, Jas. You and I are going for a bit of a walk.'

Jas rolled her eyes. 'Aw. Can't I have another muffin?'

'When we get back.' He walked over to the back door and handed her coat to her, then, over the top of Jas's head, he winked at Louise. She rewarded him with the sweetest of smiles.

As soon as the door closed behind them and they started

making their way along the path towards the old stable complex, his heart began to thump. 'Jas? You like Louise, don't you?'

Jas bent down to pick up a stick. 'Yeah. She's cool—and really pretty.'

No arguments from him there.

Suddenly his mouth went dry. 'How would you feel if she…if we…' heck, this was more nerve-racking than when he'd proposed to Megan '…if she was my girlfriend?' he finished in a rush.

Jas twiddled the stick in her fingers. 'Cool!' she said, suddenly smiling up at him. 'Can I have another muffin now?' And, without waiting for him, she ran off back to the house.

He shook his head as a grin spread on his face. How easy had that been? He'd been expecting tears, arguments about why couldn't he and Mummy live together again, but Jas had taken it totally in her stride. Maybe he wasn't doing such a bad job of bringing her up after all.

Then, realising he could now go back to the house and, at the very least, hug Louise in front of Jas, he started to jog. If only telling the rest of the world could be that simple and uneventful, but he didn't have to worry about that yet. For now, this was their little secret.

Ben should have suspected something was up as soon as he walked into the little newsagent's in the village to collect his morning paper. Instead of the buzz of gossip, the rustle of paper and the ding of the old-fashioned till, there was silence, only broken by the echo of the brass bell that had announced his arrival.

There were around six people in the shop and they all stopped what they were doing and looked at him.

He felt decidedly uncomfortable as he headed for the rack full of newspapers. Had he turned green overnight or grown an extra head? What was up with these people?

As he bent to pick up his usual broadsheet there was a collective gasp.

Okay, that was enough. He stood up and turned around to face them, his arms wide. 'What?'

Still, no one uttered a word but, one by one, they all looked at something behind him on the magazine and newspaper rack. Without turning round, he had a feeling that a trap door had opened underneath him and he was standing on thin air.

Slowly, he twisted round and scanned the display. The other villagers burst into motion and chatter, and more than one darted out of the shop without buying anything.

What the…?

He shut his eyes and opened them again, just to make sure he wasn't hallucinating. There was a woman he knew very well on the front of one of the tabloids, looking grim and angry with her arms crossed. Only, it wasn't Louise—it was Megan!

'LOUISE GOT HER CLAWS INTO MY MAN', the headline screamed in tall white letters on a black background. Below, were two smaller pictures, one a heart-shaped photo of him and Megan from the last summer holiday they'd shared together—graphically altered by putting a jagged rip between the two of them— and a headshot of Louise, taken from below, so it seemed as if she was looking down her nose at something.

He snatched the paper off the shelf. What the hell was Megan playing at?

What if Jasmine saw this? Or even her friends?

At first he was relieved that there only seemed to be three copies on display but, eventually, his brain kicked in and he realised that must be because the rest had been sold. He grabbed all three of them, marched up to the counter and threw a two pound coin down. He wasn't about to wait for change.

'You should be ashamed of yourself for selling such trash,' he told Mrs Green.

She gave him a stony look. 'Well, Mr Oliver, we all know Megan left a while ago, but you know what they say…'

Suddenly, he *really* didn't want to know what the mysterious 'they' had to say about anything. He turned and walked towards the door. Mrs Green raised her voice, just so he wouldn't miss her pearl of wisdom as he opened the door and exited the shop.

'There's no smoke without fire.'

CHAPTER TEN

WHAT a pity the old stable block had deteriorated so badly. Louise pushed gingerly at one of the doors. The building was huge—a double-height room with gigantic arched doors at one end, big enough to take a carriage or two. The low-ceilinged central section had enough stalls for one, two, three…ten horses.

There was a hatch in the ceiling above one of the abandoned stalls. What was upstairs? Those skylights in the steep slate-tiled roof had to be there for a reason. She was dying to find out. Or, at least, she was dying to think of something other than the email that had blithely pinged into her inbox earlier that morning, and pulling things apart and putting them back together again was a familiar displacement activity for her. Safe. Comforting. All-consuming.

In a corner she found a stepladder, obviously not authentic Georgian as it was made of aluminium. Still, it would do. She dragged it underneath the hatch and unfolded it, making sure the safety catches were in place.

She was up the steps in a shot and, when she pushed the hatch door, she was showered with dust and dirt and probably a hundred creepy-crawlies. Holding on to the ladder for support, she brushed her hair down with her free hand.

When she'd stopped coughing, she poked her head through the hole. Enough light was filtering through the streaky grey skylights for her to see a long loft, with fabulous supporting beams in the roof. She turned round to look in the other direction. Goodness, this must run the whole length of the stables. It was easily sixty feet long. Just think what a great space this would be if it was converted into a guest house.

Now she'd finished with the main house and the boathouse, she needed a new project.

Louise turned round and sat on the large, flat step on the top of the stepladder.

She already had a house full of rooms she didn't know what to do with. What on earth did she need a guest house for?

'Louise!'

That was Ben's voice. A second later, he appeared in the stable door, breathless and dishevelled.

'Up here,' she called, her skin cold and tingling as he peered into the dingy interior. He spotted her and ran to the bottom of the ladder. How was she going to tell him? How did she prepare him for the poisonous taste of her world? He was going to hate her for this.

'What are you doing…? Never mind.' He held a hand out and she used it to steady herself as she descended the ladder. He looked unusually pale and serious, his mouth a thin line. Her heart began to stammer.

'Ben? What is it? Is everything okay?'

'No! Everything is not bloody okay!' He pulled away from her, then marched to the door.

It was too late. He already knew. Just as she thought he was going to disappear out of the door, he turned and strode back towards her.

'Louise, I'm sorry. It's not you…I'm not angry with you, but I could happily throttle—'

'Ben!' He wasn't making sense, and that really wasn't like him. Cold horror dripped through her at the thought that something else—something far worse—might have happened. She swallowed. 'Start from the beginning! Is somebody hurt?'

He looked at her, a confused expression on his face, then

shook his head. 'No. But…' He pulled a folded newspaper from his back pocket and she was surprised to feel relief that her original assumption had been correct.

'It's Megan. She's outdone herself this time and I am so, so sorry…'

'Ben?'

'I just went into the newsagent's this morning and…well, there it was…and the whole village staring…'

She tried to make eye contact but he was talking to himself, reliving some memory more than he was talking to her. 'Ben!'

'And we were trying to keep it secret, for the kids…'

She grabbed him by the shoulder. 'Ben!'

He stopped mid-sentence and stared at her.

'I know.'

He blinked, then looked down at the paper in his hands.

'Toby's agent sent me an email. He has a press agency that deals with all his cuttings…' She shrugged and gave him what she hoped was an encouraging smile. 'Seems the cat is out of the bag.'

The frown lines on his forehead deepened. 'How can you be so blasé about it? Don't you know what she said about you…about me? Don't you know how she made it sound?'

Yes, she knew. She knew Megan had told the papers that she and Ben had been on the verge of a reconciliation when nasty old Louise had slunk up and stolen her man away. People would believe it. Even after it had come out that Toby had been unfaithful, the public had forgiven him and, somehow, there seemed to be an undercurrent that it had been her fault. She was too cold, too remote. Couldn't give him what he needed.

Well, they were right about that. What Toby really needed was a good kick in the pants, but she wasn't about to generate even more column inches for herself by being the one who provided it. She only cared about the smudged print on the paper if it affected how Ben felt about her, about starting something with her. Anything else was irrelevant.

'Forget it,' she said.

He stared at the paper again, then hurled it into the nearest stall. 'I can't!'

Louise thought back to her first really awful press story. It had hurt, cut deep. Nowadays she just ignored them. But Ben wasn't used to this. In one fell swoop, his ordered, stable little universe had been set on its head.

Silently, she walked over to him and put her arms round him. He was shaking with rage. She kissed him gently on the cheek, on the nose, on the lips, until he threw his arms round her and kissed her back.

It didn't matter what anyone else thought. He'd understand that eventually.

'Ben,' she whispered in his ear, 'the only thing that matters is that I love you.'

He pulled away and looked intently at her, as if he were trying to peel open the layers and look right inside her head. 'You do?'

She laughed. 'Of course I do!'

He began to smile. 'You never said so before.'

A blush crept up her cheeks. 'Well, I'm saying it now—' She took a deep breath and let out a shout that would have scared the horses, had there been any left. 'I love you, Ben Oliver.'

All of a sudden, her feet were off the ground and she was spinning round. Ben had grabbed her round the middle and was just twirling and twirling, all the time laughing in her ear. And then he kissed her, and it thrilled her to her very toes because this kiss was all about promises, about the future, about tomorrow.

When the euphoria wore off and her feet were finally on the ground again, his frown reappeared. 'What are we going to do?'

'Do? Nothing.'

'Nothing.' He repeated the word as if he didn't understand its meaning. 'What do you mean, "nothing"?'

She shrugged. 'As far as the press is concerned, we just don't comment. Any response from us will just keep the story running.'

'But I don't want people to think those things about you. It's not the truth!'

She silenced him with a kiss. 'The reporters don't care about truth. They care about the story—what's juiciest, what's going to sell more papers. The people who read that trash might think I'm a man-eating witch, but I don't care. What we think matters—what *we* believe about ourselves.'

'I know that's true, but it doesn't seem fair.'

'But that's how it is and we've just got to deal with it.' She exhaled long and hard. 'You might want to take Jas away for a few days, just in case people turn up wanting an interview or a picture. You've seen for yourself what some can be like.'

He nodded. 'I could ring up my sister in Exeter. She's back home now and could certainly have us for a few days, but you'll be here…all on your own.'

She took him by the hand and they walked out into the bright December morning, the sun so low in the sky it hadn't risen above the tops of the bare trees. 'I can deal with this—I have done for more than a decade. It's Jas who matters at the moment.'

He nodded. 'She's with a friend in the village right now. I'd better go and tell her we're off on an impromptu visit to Aunty Tammy's.'

Much as he'd like to wring Megan's neck right this very second, there were some important issues they needed to discuss. He jabbed at the doorbell of her flat for a third time and left his thumb on the button so it rang loud and long.

Nothing. And any calls he made to her mobile were going straight through to voicemail.

Why? Why had she done this? Had she not thought what sort of effect this would have on Jasmine?

No, of course she hadn't. Megan always thought of herself first and everyone else second. It had been her decision to end their marriage, her decision to leave Jasmine with him—saying she needed to learn to be a whole person herself before she could be a truly devoted mother—and now that he'd finally picked himself up and was moving on with his life, she was trying to sabotage that too.

Perhaps it was just as well he hadn't caught up with her, he thought as he climbed into his car and slammed the door. Choosing to hurt Louise had been cowardly; she was an easy target.

He put the car into gear and made the thirty minute drive back to Lower Hadwell. By the time he got back to his cottage it was almost two o'clock and he was supposed to be packing, then picking Jasmine up at three. It wasn't until he'd parked his car and walked round to the front that he noticed the figure on his doorstep. Megan was sitting on the low step, her face buried in her knees, drawing in jerky breaths.

He realised he wasn't angry with her any longer. If anything, he felt pity. How messed up must she be to think that selling her story to the papers would cause anything but a headache?

She stopped sniffing when she heard him walking towards her and raised her head to look at him. Her eyes were pink and her face was blotchy and puffy. He might feel sorry for her, but that didn't mean he was going to let her off the hook completely.

'Why, Megan?'

Her face crumpled, then she sniffed loudly again and wiped her nose with a crushed tissue. 'I spent the last two years following my heart, trying to work out what will make me happy, what will fill the hole in here—' She jabbed a finger at her chest.

Ben put his hands in his pockets. 'Well, maybe you did the right thing in leaving me. You obviously weren't happy, living here with me and Jasmine.'

She shook her head and rearranged the almost disintegrated tissue so she could use it for one last blow. 'No, I was happy— sort of. But it wasn't enough. I wanted more.' She fixed him with her clear blue eyes. 'Only I don't seem to be able to work out what *more* is.'

Welcome to the human race, honey.

He nearly always had a small packet of tissues in his pocket—
required kit with a child in tow. He fished a packet out of his
jacket and offered them to Megan, but her eyes were glazed and
she was staring off into the distance.

'And then I realised—oh, about a month ago—that not only
was I no happier than I had been when we were together, but that
I was *less* happy. The grass truly wasn't greener on the other side
of the fence.' Spotting the tissues, she reached up but, instead of
taking them from him, she clasped on to his hand. 'You're a good
man, Ben. And I was too blind to see that.'

She looked at him with large blue eyes and her breath caught
in her throat. Oh, no. He had a feeling he knew what was coming
next and he willed her not to say it. He pulled his hand away and
stuffed the packet of tissues into her fingers.

'Megan, we can't go back. You don't really love me that way
any more, not really. And I don't want to be with you by default,
because you can't find anything or anyone you like better. I
deserve *more* too.'

She pressed her lips together and nodded and a fresh batch of
tears ran down her face. She squeezed his hand. 'Yes, you do.
And I'm sorry for what I did. I suppose I got into a real state
because I was…' she struggled getting the next word out
'…jealous.' She gave him a weak smile. 'It was pretty obvious,
you know. The pair of you couldn't keep your eyes off each
other. Just…don't let her hurt you, Ben. I see the same ache in
her that I have inside me.'

No. Megan was wrong about that. Louise was stronger than
she was. But he wasn't going to stand on his own doorstep and
discuss that right now. He reached for Megan's hand and pulled
her up to stand.

Sometimes his ex-wife could seem like a force of nature—a
cyclone—twisting her way through other people's lives and
leaving destruction in her wake but, right now, she looked more
like a frightened child.

He put his arms around her and gave her a brotherly hug. 'We both deserve more, Meg. Don't you forget that.'

She nodded and kissed him softly on the cheek. 'Thanks, Ben. Jasmine is lucky to have a dad like you. And I think—' she paused to take a shuddering sniff '—she ought to stay with you for the time being. I reckon I have a few things to sort out first.'

Relief washed through him. That had to be the most mature and sensible decision Megan had made in a long time. Perhaps there was hope for her yet.

Louise found herself back in the stables after Ben had left. She could tell an idea was brewing about this place, but she just couldn't put her finger on it at present. There was no reason to redevelop this area, other than to keep herself from getting bored. But she sensed a need for a bit more logic in her plans. It was time to stop floating, to stop being pushed around like a sailing boat buffeted by the wind, and make some choices.

These stables had something to do with it, she could feel it. She shook her head and muttered to herself. New Year's Eve was the day after tomorrow—time to think about fresh starts and new beginnings. A shiver of happiness ran through her. Time to start a new relationship with a wonderful man who said he loved her.

She corrected herself quickly. That had sounded all wrong inside her head. They hadn't been just words. It wasn't just that he'd *said* it. Ben did love her. He did.

She walked round to the front of the house and took a few moments to look at the view down the river. This morning's clouds had evaporated and the river now twinkled and the cool sunshine made the windows in far-off Dartmouth glint and shimmer. Through the haze, she could even see the chain ferry endlessly crossing the river, touching first one bank and then the other.

Inside the house, the phone started to ring so she dashed in the front door and grabbed it before the answering machine kicked in.

'Hello, gorgeous.'

She had to prise the grin off her face to answer. 'Ben.'

'I just wanted to let you know that Jas and I have arrived at my sister's.'

'That's good. Did you see anyone, you know, hanging around your house?'

There was a pause. 'No photographers or anything like that.'

She breathed a sigh of relief.

'Anyway, I'm also calling to ask you out on a date.'

'A date?'

Ben laughed. 'Yes, a date. It's what men and women do when they like each other, and I've kind of taken a shine to you.'

'Like dinner and a movie kind of a date?'

'Not quite,' he said slowly. 'Perhaps it was fate that this all came out in the press. I'd wanted to ask you, but I didn't think we'd be going out in public for a while.' He paused. 'Lord Batterham is having a New Year's Ball at his home and I would like you to come with me.'

Oh. That was kind of scary. Talk about a baptism of fire.

'Louise? Are you still there?'

She glanced up at her reflection in the big hall mirror and immediately was reminded of the day of the fireworks display, of how he'd stood behind her and all of her senses had suddenly retuned themselves so they registered nothing but him.

'Yes, I'm still here,' she said quietly. 'And I would love to go to the ball with you.'

Somehow, she could hear him smiling on the other end of the line. 'Fantastic. I'll see you in two days. I can't wait.'

Once they'd said their goodbyes, Louise hugged the phone to her chest. A ball. Normally, she'd have found an excuse not to go, but she'd be there with Ben, and that would just make the whole evening seem magical.

Slowly, she replaced the phone in its cradle. When she looked in the mirror again, she was frowning. It would be magical. It would. She forced her reflection to soften.

Then why was a sense of foreboding hovering about her? Why did she feel that everything was so perfect that something absolutely, positively had to go wrong?

How Ben had volunteered to take Jas and her two younger cousins shopping he couldn't quite remember. His sister was subtle like that. Dangerous. Especially when the twin nephews in question were at that in-between age when they were too big for a pushchair but too young to behave themselves in crowded shops. He supposed it was his penance for foisting himself on Tammy like this.

One slippery little hand wriggled free from his and one small boy was suddenly running into the busy crowd in the shopping mall. He yelled for Jas to follow him, scooped the other boy up into his arms and gave chase.

Thankfully, Peter—the tearaway—was stopped in his tracks by a rather fed-up-looking man in a furry turkey costume. Confronted with over seven foot of slightly disgruntled bird, he began to cry.

Angus, who was fidgeting frantically in Ben's arms, saw that his brother was in distress and started to howl too. Great. The end to a perfect shopping trip. Tammy was going to wonder what sort of ordeal he'd put them through when he got back to her house.

He was now in grabbing distance of Peter and he hauled him up to join his brother. The turkey guy gave him a dismissive look.

'Ought to watch out where them kids are going,' he said, and waddled off.

Ben was tempted to yell something after him, but compromised by muttering, 'Aren't you past your sell-by date, mate? Christmas was almost a week ago.'

Jas giggled beside him.

'Remind me what else is on the list, Jas.'

She gave him a self-satisfied grin. 'A magazine for me and colouring books for the boys.'

Ben hefted the twins, who had obviously been overdosing on Christmas pudding, under his arms and set off back to the other end of the mall. One of the large chain of newsagents had a shop up that way and he could kill two birds with one stone.

As he walked into the magazine and newspaper section at the front of the shop, something very much like déjà vu made his skin pop into goosepimples. Although he was sure it was just tiredness, he took a quick look around the shop.

Jas was heading over to look at the magazines and, in one swift action, he grabbed her arm and steered her in the opposite direction. 'Why don't you go and look over there?' he said, pointing to the slightly older teenage magazines.

'Cool!' Jas didn't need to be told twice.

He was probably going to hate himself for buying her one of those later, but it was a far better option than letting her see the front page of one of the newspapers on the other display stand.

There, in full colour, was a picture of Megan kissing him on the cheek, accompanied by the heading: 'LOUISE FOILED IN LOVE AGAIN.' There wasn't much text, but he could make out another small picture of Louise. She seemed to be sneering.

Of course, the main photo looked much worse than the actual event—like an intimate moment between lovers.

Hell.

He couldn't let Jas see that. Surreptitiously, he wandered over to the display and pulled another paper across to hide the offending article. Then he accepted the magazine that Jas was waving at him, stopped by a pile of colouring books, grabbed a couple and headed for the till.

His blood was one degree off boiling temperature.

After paying, he grabbed a twin in each hand and bustled Jas out of the shop so fast she gave him one of her 'madam' looks.

Problem one dealt with.

Problem two? How was he going to explain this to Louise?

When another email popped in her inbox from Jason, Toby's agent, Louise just knew that her perfect little daydream had exploded. Nausea swirled her stomach and every part of her body went cold.

'Front page of today's *Daily News*,' the header read. The message was short and sweet: *Sorry, love. Jason xx.*

Her finger hovered above the mouse button. She waited a second, and then another. Finally, she squeezed her eyes shut and clicked. When she opened them again, she stopped breathing. Ben was looking awfully cosy with his ex-wife. Everything inside her seemed to melt and slide away. Blood rushed in her ears.

Think, Louise. Think. Don't just react.

She tipped her head to one side. A pointless gesture. It wasn't going to look any better from a different angle. But she forced herself to remember the hundreds of photos she'd seen of herself in the past, all seeming to tell a true story when a split second taken out of context could tell so many lies.

Ben had said he loved her.

And she'd seen the way he was with Megan. He tolerated her, nothing more.

She closed the file but a ghost of the photograph lingered, a trick of the light, so she got up and walked to the window. She'd thought those days were behind her—the dread each morning when she watched the news or walked past a paper stand. And she'd never thought she'd have to worry about that with Ben. But then, she'd wanted him, and having him meant dragging him into her world and dealing with the consequences. It was more pressure than a fledgling relationship should have to take.

Ninety-nine per cent of her knew there was nothing to worry about. But too many years of looking over her shoulder, of second-guessing everything the man in her life did, had left her wary. And that one per cent was like an itch she couldn't help scratching. What if...?

She pressed her forehead against the cold glass and let her breath steam the window. Wishes and dreams were all very well when they stayed inside your head but, once they crossed the threshold into the real world, they were fragile, vulnerable—like the paper-thin glass baubles on a Christmas tree.

What was wrong with her? Hadn't she wanted someone to look at her the way Ben looked at her? To see right inside her?

But there was her problem. Daydream Louise had been her better self, her angel. When Real Louise looked deep down to see what Ben saw, it wasn't comfortable at all. No sugar, no spice, no all things nice. Just fear and loneliness and broken parts of the person she'd once been that she didn't know how to fix. And if Ben couldn't see all that, maybe he wasn't *really* seeing her after all.

Abruptly, she pulled away from the window. Stop it! You'll make yourself crazy playing mind games like this.

The crunch of boots on the gravel outside had her spinning round and pressing herself against the window once again. For the second time that day, she couldn't quite believe what she was seeing.

Ben?

He was supposed to be in Exeter.

She flattened a palm against the window, wanting to reach out to him, but glad the barrier was in place. Her movement must have caught his eye because he suddenly spotted her there and walked straight towards her.

His eyes said it all. *Believe me.*

Pinned by his gaze, she stood motionless as he raised his hand and pressed it against the outside of the window, covering the outline of her hand completely. She studied it, then let her eyes meet his again.

Let me in, they said.

Wordlessly, she peeled her hand away and moved towards the study door. Ben mirrored her and when she opened the heavy panelled front door he was standing there, waiting. Now, with no transparent barrier between them, they both hesitated. It was Ben who broke the silence.

'I can explain.'

She almost didn't need the words. His face told her everything she needed to know. The pain etched there broke her heart and she wrapped her arms around his neck and pulled him to her. He gave no resistance and walked into her arms, burying his face in the hollow of her neck. 'I'm sorry,' he whispered against her skin. 'She came to apologise. I was careless.'

She nodded, her chin butting into his shoulder. 'Why are you here? Where's Jas?'

He took a step back and steadied himself—or was it her?—by placing a hand on each of her shoulders.

'She's with my sister. Believe me, I'm heavily in debt in the babysitting stakes. But I had to see you, to know you were okay.'

He smoothed the hair away from her face with such tenderness. Her eyes began to tingle and fill. 'I'm okay. We're okay. It just…shook me for a moment.'

Colour that she hadn't realised had been missing returned to his face and his whole body seemed to exhale. She tried a shaky smile and it seemed to work.

'Come on,' she said. 'Let's do something normal. How about a cup of tea?'

Ben began to laugh. 'Please, no. Anything but that! I finally think I've drunk my fill.'

'We'll have to switch to coffee, then. You go ahead and put the kettle on. There's something I've got to do.'

He looked over his shoulder twice as he disappeared down the hall to the kitchen, and she watched him until he disappeared. Then she nipped into the study, highlighted Jason's email and deleted it.

As she turned to leave, she spotted Ben's palm print on the window. She felt it must mean something, but she didn't know what, and that bothered her. Some vital piece of information was missing, something she needed to know but couldn't yet. And that just made the *one per cent* of doubt tickle all the harder.

CHAPTER ELEVEN

THE lanes wound so tightly as he neared Whitehaven that Ben had to slow the car to a crawl. In places only an ancient stone wall separated the road from a steep hill that fell away into the river. Tall pines and beeches towered overhead and, even if the moon had deigned to glimpse from behind a cloud, it wouldn't have illuminated much.

The road dipped halfway down the hill, signalling the descent that led to Whitehaven's main gate, and Ben's stomach dipped with it. The last week had been an emotional roller coaster ride, yet those seven short days now felt like a lifetime.

Cold swirled around him—not from the vents; they were blasting warm air. It was just the physical reaction he seemed to have every time he thought about how he might have lost Louise. He never wanted to feel that way again.

In the drive from Exeter to see her, he'd felt completely un-hitched from any point in reality. She turned him inside out and upside down. And, a couple of months ago, he would have thought that a bad thing.

Perhaps he was going insane. That would certainly account for the small satin-covered box in his pocket. It would make sense of the square-cut diamond nestled within. Just like a magpie, he hadn't been able to resist it when he'd seen it in the jeweller's window. Not that he was going to do anything with it yet. It was far too soon. It was just with him for safe-keeping. For luck.

And, besides, he had another, less conventional gift for her. One that would leave her with no shadow of a doubt that she was the only one in his heart. It was a gamble, but he wasn't prepared to sit down in defeat as Louise had. He'd decided to fight—for them. For her.

Amidst the shifting shapes of the wind-blown branches, his headlights fell upon the thick vertical posts of Whitehaven's gates. The level drive traversed the hill with only a slight curve. He squeezed his foot on the accelerator. Not that he was late; just because he needed to.

He parked right outside the front door. The gravel drive was probably murder to negotiate in high heels. Feeling as nervous as a sixteen-year-old on his first proper date, he eased himself from the car and rang the bell. No one came. It was only as he reached for it a second time that he noticed the small note taped underneath it: '*Come inside. L x.*'

Now his heart really started to race. Stop it, he told himself. There's no need for this. You're not going to say anything…ask anything…tonight. It's too early.

He entered the marble-tiled hallway and paused. 'Louise?'

'Up here.' Her voice drifted down through the crystals in the hanging chandelier. 'I'll be one more minute.'

Now, the untrained observer would have expected a woman like Louise to keep him waiting, but it didn't surprise him in the least when, almost exactly sixty seconds later, he heard a door open upstairs and the swish of expensive fabric on the landing.

At first he couldn't see her properly. The glittering crystals in the chandelier distorted his view. But, as she reached the top of the stairs and started to descend, he got the whole picture.

He couldn't say anything. He couldn't smile. Heck, he couldn't even breathe.

The dress was long and the shade of midnight, in some heavy, shiny fabric that flared slightly as it fell to her ankles. And her hair…it was held in glossy waves and pinned up at the back, just like a nineteen-twenties movie star.

'You look stunning,' he managed to mutter as she reached the foot of the stairs and smiled at him. Just as well he got that out before she turned round and revealed the impossibly low back.

Unfortunately, he needed to go to this party to keep Lord Batterham sweet, otherwise he'd have been tempted to see if that satin was as soft as it looked, if it would fall off her shoulders easily and ripple as it slid to her feet.

She gave him a sweet, sexy smile as she wound a wrap around her shoulders. 'You don't look too bad yourself, either. I must say, for the gardener, you scrub up pretty good.'

Pretty good? He'd show her.

Before she could back away, he caught her in his arms and showed her just how *good* he could be.

That horrible scratchy feeling that had plagued her for the last day or so had finally disappeared. She hadn't noticed when it had subsided, all she knew was that standing here, in the grand ballroom of Batterham Hall, with Ben at her side, the magic was alive and spinning again.

As the minute hand on the ridiculously ornate clock crept towards midnight, she felt as if she'd emerged from under a huge cloud. Finally, the past was behind her and she could look forward again. And not just to tomorrow, but beyond and beyond and beyond.

She'd been quite relieved to discover that half of Lord Batterham's guests had no idea who she was. Apparently, *Buzz* magazine wasn't popular reading amongst the upper crust. And, although she'd thought she'd find some of these people stuffy and aloof, she'd warmed to many of the people she'd met.

And there was Ben. Always there. Always anticipating what she needed before she opened her mouth to express it. Not in the annoying, sycophantic way some people did, but just in his own unique matter-of-fact, *I knew you needed it, so I got it* kind of way. His impeccable manners were making him a huge hit—she half-suspected there were a couple of elderly duchesses who were plotting to steal him away.

The orchestra—not a string quartet or a band, but a full orchestra—finished their piece and paused while the master of ceremonies announced a waltz to take them up to midnight, now only five minutes away.

Ben, who had cleverly managed to be otherwise engaged for most of the dancing, now swung her into his arms and struck the appropriate pose.

'Ben, I know you're wonderful, but do mind this dress with those great feet of yours. It's vintage Chanel.'

'My feet will behave themselves impeccably,' he said without a trace of irony, even though he'd managed to stamp on her toes at least ten times already this evening. Gardening, yes. Dancing, no. But somehow that just made him all the more adorable.

'I've been practising this one,' he said proudly. 'I wanted to learn more but Gaby, Luke's wife, refused to teach me anything else. She said this was all I'd be able to handle.'

God bless Gaby, thought Louise, as they started to move around the floor.

But, as they continued to move, he surprised her. Okay, he wouldn't win any competitions, but she stopped being terrified for her dress and started to enjoy herself. Round and round they went, circling the vast ballroom. Was this what it felt like—to have all your dreams come true? Because, right at this moment, she was living in a fairy tale.

The music began to fade and it took her a couple of seconds to realise that the musicians were actually ending the waltz, not that everything but she and Ben was melting away into a dream world.

The first shout made her jump. 'Ten…'

She looked at Ben, who was grinning, obviously pretty pleased with himself.

'Nine…eight…' the chant around them continued.

'What?' she asked, starting to smile.

'Seven…six…five…'

He nodded upwards and bent his head back to look towards the ceiling. They were standing directly underneath a large display of greenery, dripping with bright white lights and, tied at the bottom with a sumptuous red bow, was a generous sprig of mistletoe.

She laughed, then quickly went silent as a very serious look appeared in Ben's eyes—one that made her knees tremble and her heart rate double.

'Four…three…two…'

'One,' he said, then delivered a kiss that shook her to the toes of her sparkly shoes. The cheering and clapping and congratulating carried on around them, but it was as if she and Ben were in their own separate bubble.

Were you allowed to make wishes at New Year, or was that only on birthdays and when stars fell? Because she wished that it could always be like this—total perfection, just like her dreams.

When Ben ended the kiss, she couldn't bear to open her eyes. Instead, she threw her arms around his neck and hugged him tight enough to make her arm muscles shake. Pressed right up against his chest, she could feel his heart beating, racing even faster than her own.

He kissed the tip of her earlobe and a shudder ran through her. Then he whispered in her ear.

'Marry me?'

She froze. All around her the dream began to splinter. And she had no idea why, because that question should have been the perfect prelude to a happy ever after. She only knew she was terrified out of her wits. This was *too* real, *too*…much.

'Louise?' There was a shake in his voice and she hated the fact that she'd put it there. She pulled away from him and smoothed down the antique satin of her dress. 'I think we should leave,' she said, unable to look at him. She was angry with herself for hurting him and, perhaps a little unreasonably, angry at him too.

Ben ran after her as she marched off to the cloakroom and retrieved her wrap. She could tell he was itching to talk to her, but there were too many people around. And, coward that she was, she was glad.

Within five minutes they were in the warm of his car, pulling out of the gates of Batterham Hall and weaving down the country lanes back towards home.

'It's too fast, isn't it?' Ben finally said grimly. 'I got carried away.'

'Are you saying you didn't mean it?'

'No! I mean…no,' he said in a quieter tone. 'I would never play with your feelings that way.'

Not intentionally. But men were apt to promise the world when they were swept up in the first flush of love. Toby had been the same. It didn't mean it was going to last a lifetime. Just at the hint of the possibility that it wouldn't, her stomach turned to ice. Oh, she really didn't understand what was going on inside her head this evening!

She did her best to explain it to Ben, staring at her lap mostly and only risking the odd glance across at him as he drove. 'It's all so new. How can we possibly tell what we are really feeling? We're riding the first wave of infatuation and we need to leave ourselves time to get past that.' There. That sounded much more reasonable.

He took his eyes off the road and turned his head sharply to look at her. 'You think I'm just infatuated with you?'

She'd made him angry. That hadn't been her intention at all. He glared at her for a hard second, then returned his attention to the road. An instant denial should have popped out of her mouth by now, shouldn't it?

'No,' she said slowly.

'I'm not just infatuated with you, Louise.'

Suddenly, he swung into a passing place on the narrow road and wrenched the handbrake on. He reached upwards and flicked a switch for a small light on the inside roof of the car. She swallowed. She'd always sensed that beneath the down-to-earth, practical exterior, Ben was a man who cared passionately and felt deeply. She just hadn't expected it all to burst to the surface tonight.

He turned to stare out of the windscreen. 'Maybe I am a little bit infatuated, if thinking that everything about you is amazing, if wanting to spend my whole future with you fits the definition. I thought I'd found the woman who was my other half…'

Unshed tears clogged her throat. They were wonderful words, but if she picked them apart just a little…

Everything about her definitely wasn't amazing, and that told her she was more right than she wanted to be. They *did* need more time. Why couldn't he see that?

He turned just his head to face her, and his eyes were burning. 'It's more than that, Louise.'

She shook her head. 'You can't know that for sure. Not yet.'

His mouth settled into a grim line. 'You're wrong. I know what I feel, what I want. I've never been more certain. It's *you* that doesn't know for sure.'

How could she know? Real life wasn't like daydreams or the movies when it all became obvious in a blinding split-second. She'd felt this way before and she'd been spectacularly wrong. Of course she wasn't sure!

'You don't have any faith in me,' he said grimly as he put the car into gear and drove away.

Louise was pushing him away as hard as she could and it was his own stupid fault. He'd been hasty—which really wasn't like him—even so, he was one hundred per cent certain that she was wrong about the infatuation thing. And he'd prove it to her somehow. First of all, he had to find out what was behind all of this. Something had triggered Louise's panic button. Somehow, he'd touched on a really raw nerve.

When they arrived at her house, he insisted on accompanying her inside, sure that if he left it now, she would retreat inside her shell and he might not have the opportunity again. He had to talk to her now while it was all brimming at the surface.

She wasn't pleased about him being there, he could tell. An air of irritation hung about her as she led him into the drawing room and poured him a miserly brandy. He took a seat across the room from her as she perched on a dark purple velvet sofa.

'Why can't you believe, Louise? What's happened that makes it so difficult for you to trust your feelings?'

She took a deep breath and he saw her shutters rise. Damn! For five long minutes she stared into the cold fireplace. Then, still keeping her gaze locked on it, she said, 'I'm scared to. I so want it to be real, Ben.'

Instantly, he was across the room and sitting beside her. There were wounds here that were too old, too deep to be healed in a moment. He'd been a fool. If he'd realised they were there, he would have trodden a lot more carefully. But she'd seemed so different recently, happier, freer...

She leaned against him, but still continued to stare into the empty fireplace. He placed an arm lightly round her shoulders and stroked the soft skin of her upper arm with his fingers. She didn't push him away. It was no longer about convincing her, getting her to see the truth. For now, the important thing was just that she get a chance to vent things that had been buried for too long.

He waited, knowing that pushing her with questions might easily make her re-erect the defences.

When she spoke, her voice was so soft he had to strain to hear it. 'Right from when I was very young, life was about putting other people first—which isn't a bad thing. Don't get me wrong. But even when I didn't want to, I had no choice. So I used to daydream about the life I couldn't have while I was being mother to my younger brothers and sisters and taking care of my father.' She turned to look at him and his heart broke to see her eyes full of such pain. 'I suppose it was my survival mechanism.'

'We all have those,' he said tenderly.

She turned back and he guessed she found it easier not to look at him.

'Well, one day,' she continued, 'someone walked up to me and offered me all my dreams wrapped up in a sparkly box with a big bow—fame, success, recognition, enough money so I'd never have to worry about not having any clothes except my school uniform, enough money so I wouldn't see the little ones' eyes when I served up beans on toast for tea again…And love. I thought I'd found love.'

He sighed. Louise had had the kind of childhood he worked his hardest to protect Jasmine from. He thought of this brave woman, not much older than his daughter, running a household, studying, caring for a sick relative. Who would blame her for reaching for the dream?

'And so I was selfish. I chose something for myself.' She buried her face in her hands and the tears came thick and fast. Ben hugged her tight and kissed the top of her head. He knew exactly who would blame her for such a thing—she blamed herself. One by one the puzzle pieces clicked into place, fragments of things she'd told him that suddenly made sense—her relationship with Toby, her father, why she continued to punish herself.

'You can't blame yourself for your father's death, you know. From what you've told me, he was a very sick man.'

Okay, maybe he could have phrased that a little better, because Louise broke down completely. She was crying so hard she could hardly breathe, let alone speak. Years of guilt and pain, of grieving she had never allowed herself to do, came spilling out in one go. He hugged her fiercely, as if he could protect her from it by sheer strength.

Through the sobs she croaked, 'But I…shouldn't have… left him!'

People thought she'd stuck with Toby all those years because she wanted the glitz and glamour more than she wanted her self-respect. How wrong they were. It came to him with crystal clarity: Louise had stayed with Toby because she believed she deserved him. He was her penance.

Then a second thunderbolt hit. That wonderful New Year's surprise he'd had planned for Louise. It was the worst possible thing he could have done.

Louise opened one eye. Stark light sliced through the windows, bearing testimony to the fact that she'd been too exhausted to remember to draw the curtains when she'd crawled upstairs in the small hours of the morning.

Her eyes, her head, even her throat ached. Nerves tickled her tummy. She had that awful sick feeling in her stomach. Too many emotions, too many tears. She wanted to call it all back and pretend it hadn't happened. What must Ben think of her now?

At the thought of him, she raised herself on one elbow. Last time she'd seen him he was curling up on the sofa with a blanket—which was completely ridiculous as she had at least ten empty bedrooms—but he'd insisted.

She got out of bed and her foot met something slippery and incredibly smooth. Her Chanel dress lay in a heap where she'd let it drop before falling into bed. She picked it up and draped it over a low upholstered chair in the corner before wandering into her bathroom and having a shower.

There was no noise from downstairs when she emerged. Yesterday morning she'd have been rushing downstairs to meet him. Today she wasn't even sure she wanted to see Ben. He'd pushed her too far, made her feel things she wasn't ready to feel. And, while she knew he'd had the best intentions in the world, that didn't mean she wasn't cross with him.

In her mind, she played out the argument she wanted to have with him, telling him to back off and leave her alone. Who did he think he was, dragging all that stuff out of her? What gave him the right?

She walked to the dressing table and picked up a comb and untangled her hair with unforgiving strokes.

When she could delay it no longer she padded down the sweeping staircase, dressed in a grey track suit and large pink slippers. The echoing silence made it seem colder than it really was and she crossed her arms across her chest and hugged herself.

She found a note in the kitchen: *'Be back soon. Something I have to sort out. Ben.'*

She scrunched it into a little ball and threw it in the bin. Then, while the kettle boiled, she rehearsed the coming argument in her head again. Who had given him the job of deciding what she needed? *She* ought to be what she needed, and she certainly didn't need some man to step into the slot Toby had left and take over her life. Okay, Ben wasn't the same. He was full of concern rather than apathy, but that didn't make her feel any less overruled, overshadowed.

As she drained the last of her cup of tea, she heard a knock at the back door and turned to see Ben standing there, his face grim. Outside, she might have looked as if she didn't care if he was there or not. Inside, she was seething. She walked over, opened the door, then walked away again before he could touch her.

He stepped into the kitchen and rested against the counter without removing his coat. 'I have something to confess.'

She almost laughed. What now? He had another wife, a spare one, raving mad and locked in the attic? That would just about be her luck. She retreated to the opposite side of the kitchen, crossed her arms and raised her eyebrows.

'I had arranged a meeting with a journalist for this week. I was going to give an interview about…us.'

Louise felt her jaw drop.

He closed his eyes and shook his head, just once. 'I know, I know. At the time I thought I was doing the right thing.' He opened his eyes and looked at her. All the carefully rehearsed lines of her row trickled away. 'I wanted to fight for you, to tell the world what a wonderful person you are, that you're not what everybody thinks you are…I wanted them all to see what I see.'

It was very noble. It was also very stupid.

'I'm not going to do it now,' he said. 'I cancelled the meeting.'

'Well, thank you so much for telling me.' The level of sarcasm in her voice surprised even her.

'Don't be like that.'

'Why not, Ben? Why shouldn't I be angry that you decided all on your own what was best for me? You should have talked it through with me.' She placed her hands on her hips and shook her head slowly from side to side. 'This is becoming a pattern, you know—you jumping in and rescuing me from myself. Well, you know what? Perhaps I don't need rescuing!'

He stood up and walked towards her. 'It's not like that, Louise. I love you.'

She backed away, still shaking her head. 'I'm not one of your stupid plants, you know, something to be trained or cultivated. You can't fix me, Ben. I am who I am and you need to accept that—all of that—and if you can't, then perhaps I don't need you at all.'

Ben stopped walking and stared at her. How could he convince her? 'I know I messed up, Louise. And I know I jumped in too fast, but that's only because…I've never felt this way about anyone else—ever. It excites me, confuses me, scares the life out of me. I don't want to lose you.'

Her shutters fell again, and this time they were clamped down and double bolted. With an increasing sick feeling in his gut, he realised that this was the kickback from last night. She was too raw, and she was protecting herself the only way she knew how.

The Louise he knew would never hold a grudge about that stupid magazine interview. It was just easier for her to feel anger, to hate him for that, than to let herself feel any of the other things last night's conversation had brought up. And he wasn't going to get anywhere by pushing. He had made that spectacularly awful mistake already and it had triggered this whole mess.

But he was going to leave her in no doubt as to how he felt about her before he gave her the space she needed. She had to believe him about that. Knowing she would just retreat if he approached her, he stayed rooted to the spot and hoped the truth of his words could pierce her shield.

He wanted to say something beautiful, elegant, poetic—something to reflect just a tiny bit of what he felt for her—but his mind was blank. No flowery words seemed to measure up. So he spoke with his eyes, his body, his whole being and, finally, he simply said, 'I love you. I always will.'

The shield around her buckled just enough for him to see a deep yearning ache behind the fire in her eyes. She wanted to believe him, but she was too scared, and he tried to pinpoint why that was. What was the overriding factor here?

Guilt.

The word popped into his head as if someone had whispered it in his ear.

The irony of it all hit him like a blow in the solar plexus. Once again, he was offering all he had—his heart, his life, his love— to a woman, and it wasn't enough. While she nursed her guilt, anything he could give her, even if he wrapped the whole universe up and put it in a silver box, would never be enough.

Until she believed she deserved the happy ever after she yearned for so desperately, it would always be out of her reach. Until she understood she was worth being loved, she would always doubt him. Always. And that tiny speck of doubt, like a grain of sand would irritate and irritate until she couldn't stand it any more. Even if he could talk her round now, their relationship would die from a slow-acting poison.

He had to let her go. Just the thought of that made his nose burn and his eyes sting. He coughed the sensation away.

Louise was looking at him with a strange mix of irritation and confusion on her face. It took all his strength not to reach for her, not to taste her lips one last time. Heavy steps took him across the kitchen to the door. He opened it, stepped through, then turned to take one last look.

'Goodbye, Louise,' he said, then closed the door and walked away.

The daffodils were gone and blossom was on the trees when work on the old stable block was completed. The garden was looking fabulous too, although that always made her feel a little sad. Ben's men had done a grand job. She hadn't seen him again, really, since New Year's Day. She kept away from the village, preferring to shop in the nearby towns, although she fancied she'd seen him from a distance a few times. On each occasion she'd turned tail and scurried away.

How could she face him? After all those awful things she'd said to him? She'd had a chance and she'd blown it. More than that. She'd blasted it to smithereens with dynamite.

At least she'd found something to do to take her mind off it all.

She'd spent most of January unpacking her feelings about her childhood. In her teenage years she'd just soldiered on, doing the best she could. But now, looking back on her past with the eyes of a mother, she wondered why there hadn't been more help. Social Services had been very keen to let them know when things weren't up to scratch, but nobody had ever offered to step in and help.

A break—just a week away from it now and then—might have made all the difference. She'd have gone back refreshed, ready to carry on. And she'd have been less susceptible to impossible fairy tales and knights. Not a knight in shining armour, but in black leather—wolves' clothing. She sighed. Maybe that was being unfair to Toby. He wasn't the devil incarnate; he was just immature, weak, spoiled.

Louise picked up her bunch of keys and headed out towards

the stables. It was time for one last look around before her guests arrived.

In the small cobbled courtyard in front of the stables there was now a fountain and bright flowers in pots, benches to sun oneself on. Inside was even better. Four apartments, which she'd really enjoyed decorating, had all the mod cons, everything needed for a week of relaxation and pampering.

As winter had faded and the snowdrops had appeared on the hillside, she'd approached Relief, a charity that specialised in giving respite care for young people who had to act as carers for sick or disabled family members. They were desperate for more locations to send the kids, places they could rest, unwind and meet others in the same boat. On site would be a cook and general den-mother, so the guests didn't have to do chores and cooking as they did at home, and a child psychologist would be making regular visits.

She took one last look around the apartments, checking everything was perfect. Three girls and a boy were due to arrive from London in the next hour. She plumped a cushion on one of the settees in the communal sitting room, which led on to the dining room and kitchen. She was getting too emotional about this, she knew, but she just wanted these kids to have the best. They deserved it.

CHAPTER TWELVE

BY THE end of the week, the occupants of the new apartments had stopped staring every time they saw her and were much more ready to beg for cake or tease her. Jack was really enjoying having the company too. He'd been itching for Saturday when he'd be able to join in the fun. He and Kate, the den mother, had taken three of their 'guests'—James, Letitia and Rebecca—on a guided tour of the grounds. Not that they hadn't explored every square inch already. But, apparently, only Jack knew all the best trees for climbing.

Only Molly had remained behind. She was a quiet, mousy girl who had only hovered on the fringes of the group all week. Louise found her in the stable courtyard when she went to collect a cake tin she'd left in the kitchen.

'Hey, Molly! How's it going?'

Molly dipped her head and looked at Louise through her thick, dark blonde hair. 'Okay.'

'Have you been having a good time?'

Molly grimaced. 'Yes.' She fidgeted. 'Can I phone home?'

Louise sat down next to her. The spring air was sweet and fresh and the sun was beautifully warm on her skin in the sheltered courtyard. If she sat here for more than a few minutes, she'd have to take her cardigan off.

'Of course you can. But I thought you already called this morning.'

Molly nodded and looked away.

'They're okay, you know—your family. They'll do fine while you're here. Relief will have sent some excellent staff to do all your usual jobs while you're away.'

Molly looked unconvinced. 'They might not do things right. I need to check.'

Louise dearly wanted to put her arm round the girl, but she wasn't sure it would be welcomed. Only fourteen, and already she carried the responsibility for her two disabled parents. The psychologist had warned her that some of the children might be like this.

'How would you like something to do?'

At this, Molly brightened. Just as Louise had guessed, she would feel less uncomfortable…less guilty…if she had a job to do.

'You lot are eating cakes faster than I can bake them. I was planning to do a chocolate one today and I could do with an extra pair of hands.'

For the first time that week, Molly smiled. 'Sure. I can help.'

As they measured and mixed and washed up back in Whitehaven's kitchen, Molly began to relax a little. Louise took the opportunity to dispense a little wisdom.

'It's okay to enjoy yourself, you know.'

Molly frowned. 'I know that.'

Hoping that this would be the right time, she walked over to her and put an arm gently round her shoulders. 'You don't have to feel guilty for being here, for having a nice time. It's what the scheme is all about.'

Molly sniffed. 'I know that. It's just that I feel bad leaving Mum and Dad alone while I get to stay in a beautiful place like this…and with you. It's too nice.'

One-handed, Louise tore a piece of kitchen towel off the roll on the table and handed it to the girl. 'Molly…' Oh, blow, she was tearing up too. She grabbed a piece for herself as well. 'You work hard all year round. Much harder than other kids your age.

You deserve this, you really do. And your parents would want you to enjoy yourself while you're here, not spend the whole time worrying about them or feeling guilty.'

As she hugged Molly, she could suddenly picture her own father's face the day she'd run home from the supermarket and told him about the modelling scout. He'd been so proud of her! And never once had he said anything to make her feel as if she was abandoning him. He'd been such a special man.

And yet, for all these years, she'd held on to the same feeling that was eating Molly alive. The girl beside her started to tremble and Louise pulled her close for a proper hug. 'Is it really okay?' Molly whispered.

'Yes.' The kitchen distorted and became all blurry. Louise's lip began to wobble. 'Yes, it is.'

Ben walked into Mrs Green's shop on a crisp May morning to get his usual paper. She'd been as meek as a lamb with him since that incident at Christmas. Louise now had a most loyal supporter in her. And that was good. For Louise. The tide of opinion might turn one person at a time, but it was still turning in the right direction.

Thoughts of Louise led to thoughts of Whitehaven and its luscious gardens. He would have loved to have seen how the gardens had turned out, if they matched the vision in his head when he'd drawn up the plans. Best of all would be the places he hadn't touched, the woods full of foxgloves and bluebells. Sometimes you had to know when to stop meddling and let things be, to let them retain their natural beauty.

He reached the counter and Mrs Green just handed him a paper without asking which one. Then she handed him a glossy women's magazine, not one of the cheap, gossipy ones, but one of the high-fashion mags that also ran articles on serious subjects.

'A bit old for Jas, Mrs Green,' he said, without looking at it, and handed it back to her.

She shook her head. 'I thought you might be interested.'

Him? He started to chuckle, but a glimpse of a pair of dark and stormy eyes on the cover made him look a little closer. Louise. She'd done an interview. He moved out of the way of the counter so the person behind him could pay and scrabbled through the pages until he found the article he was looking for. It was a long one.

He read it as he walked down the hill back to the cottage. He was working from home today. More than once he stopped in the middle of the road and shook his head. Especially when he realised he'd forgotten to pay Mrs Green. She'd understand. Then he started to smile, even though the ache in his chest that he thought had dulled a little in the last few months began to quietly throb again.

Amazing. He'd always said so. And here she was believing it. Living it.

Not only had she done something amazing at Whitehaven, she was doing the interview to raise the profile of the charity she was now patron of. Relief were lobbying the Government for new funding for child carers, not just respite care but proper practical help on a day-to-day basis.

And Louise Thornton, the woman who would rather cut off her right arm than talk to a journalist, had not only given an interview—and let the photographers into the new apartments at Whitehaven—but had opened up about her own childhood, her own lack of education, in an effort to prevent more children from living through the same things. He felt his chest expand as he read that she was planning to study part-time for a degree in child psychology.

He reached his front door and misjudged putting the key in the lock because he just couldn't stop reading. He flicked the magazine closed so he could stare at the cover. Yes, the eyes were dark and intense, as always, but they were no longer empty.

This could be the stupidest thing he'd ever done. Apart from jumping the gun on New Year's Eve, that was. Ben tied his dinghy on to the iron ring outside Louise's boathouse and wondered whether he should just sail straight back across the river because, actually, he'd been right the first time. This *was* the stupidest thing he'd ever done.

It was just past noon and the most glorious summer day. He stood for a moment on the jetty and considered his next move. Where was Louise likely to be at this time of day?

It saddened him that he didn't know, that her life had changed so much since he'd last seen her. But at the same time he was immensely proud of her. He'd seen all that potential inside of her, but it took strength of character and guts to turn that into something real.

Something flashed up on the boathouse balcony and he immediately craned his neck to see what it was. The sun had bounced off the glass part of the door as it had opened and out stepped…Louise.

She was wearing a faint smile and her long chocolate-brown hair glowed chestnut in the sunshine. He couldn't move, suddenly didn't know what to say. If it was possible, he'd forgotten how beautiful she was—or maybe she had just got more beautiful, because there was something different about her.

She rested her hands on the edge of the balcony and leaned forward, breathing in the salty river air.

And then she saw him and stiffened in surprise. He couldn't hear her from where he was standing, but he was sure he saw her mouth his name. The lapping of the river, the constant shrieking of the seagulls all died away as they both stood frozen to the spot, staring at each other.

She smiled. And then he was running—up the jetty, up the steps to the boathouse's upper room. He made himself stop when he got to the door that led on to the narrow balcony, half worried she would disappear into thin air if he got too close.

She was leaning against the rail, her back to the river. Her long, frilly-edged skirt fidgeted in the breeze. 'Ben,' she repeated.

Her smile was soft and warm, with a hint of sadness. 'It's good to see you again.'

He nodded. Nothing sensible was going to come out of his mouth unless he got his act together. 'You too.'

His heart started to pound in his chest as he crossed the threshold on to the balcony. He was close enough to touch her now, but he wouldn't—not yet.

'I saw the article in the magazine.'

Okay. If this was as smooth as he was going to get, he might just as well jump back into his dinghy right now.

She nodded. 'I'm going to be in the spotlight whether I like it or not, so I might as well get to choose where it shines.' She looked at her feet, then back up at him. 'So, Ben Oliver, why are you trespassing on my land again after all this time?'

It was a joke and he was supposed to laugh, but he seemed to have lost the knack.

'I…um…forgot to give you something.'

She frowned and her eyebrows arched in the middle. 'When?'

'At Christmas.'

His heart slunk into his boots. On the way over here this had seemed clever, now it just seemed…lame.

'Christmas was a long time ago.'

He reached into his pocket and his fingers closed around the palm-sized box hidden there. 'I know. But some gifts have their own seasons. This one was a little early back then.'

She bit her lip. 'Am I going to like this gift?'

It was now or never. And he was shaking in his sensible boots. He looped the little ribbon holding the box closed round his finger and used it to pull the silver parcel out of his pocket. Then he dropped it in her hands.

'I'm not sure it's in season even now, but sometimes…you can just…wait too long…'

It didn't seem to matter that he wasn't making any sense, because she was staring so hard at the little package he sensed she wasn't taking it in anyway. With excruciating slowness, she tugged the velvet bow and let it fall to the floor. Then she pulled the lid off the box.

'Oh.'

Oh? Was that a good 'oh' or a bad 'oh'?

'Oh, Ben!'

A good 'oh'. Warmth began to spread upwards from his toes.

Her nose crinkled in confusion. 'Mistletoe? But it's almost summer!' Gently, she reached into the box and pulled the sprig out to look at it. A thin white ribbon looped round the top and was tied in an elaborate bow. 'It's not even plastic! It's…'

'…the real deal,' he finished for her.

She stepped close enough for him to smell her perfume. 'How did you…?'

He shrugged. 'I have my sources.'

She twiddled the mistletoe between finger and thumb and suddenly grew more serious. 'What does this mean, Ben?'

'Isn't it obvious?'

She bit her lip and looked away. 'You want to…kiss me?'

Always. For ever. But he'd promised himself he wouldn't until she'd given him the answer he wanted to hear. 'I love you, Louise. I always will.'

Louise shook her head. 'After all the things I said to you! I don't deserve it!'

He couldn't use his hands to make her look at him, so he concentrated on just pulling her gaze to his by the force of his willpower. 'Yes, you do.'

Six months ago, he would have seen the doubt in her eyes, but the woman standing before him looked deep into his eyes and he saw the light of recognition flicker on. Slowly, she raised her arm so the little green sprig dangled above her head and, taking a deep breath, she closed her eyes.

This was it. Now or never. He thought perhaps he was going to hyperventilate, but managed to pull himself together. Louise was still poised, ready for the kiss, her lips soft and slightly parted. When he didn't respond straight away, she lifted one eyelid, making the other scrunch up.

Her whisper of uncertainty only made his fingers shake all the more. 'Ben?'

He nodded up to the little green sprig with its cluster of white berries above their heads. 'Look a little closer.'

With his fingers as deft as a bunch of bananas, he tugged her hand downward so the mistletoe rested at eye level and she could see the diamond ring held fast by the white velvet bow.

'Marry me?'

Louise's eyes snapped all the way open and she dropped the sprig on the floor, then her hands flew to her chest and stayed there.

His heart tap-danced inside his ribcage. He bent down and gently rescued both mistletoe and ring before he trampled it with his boots. Louise looked as if she was in a trance. Taking a chance, because she wasn't slapping him in the face or running up the hill, he twirled the mistletoe above their heads once more.

'Please…?'

'Yes! Oh, Ben, yes!' She threw herself at him and almost sent him flying over the edge of the balcony. He guided her hands so she gently pulled at the ribbon to release the ring and it dropped into his waiting hand.

She looked up at him, laughing and shaking her head, her eyes shining. 'Are you for real, Ben Oliver?'

He nodded and lowered his head, then brushed his mouth across hers, savouring the moment, and slid the ring on to her left hand. 'Merry Christmas, Louise,' he whispered against her lips, before wrapping her in his arms and pulling her into the cool darkness of the boathouse.

Silhouette®

SPECIAL EDITION™

**FROM *NEW YORK TIMES*
BESTSELLING AUTHOR**

LINDA LAEL MILLER

A STONE CREEK CHRISTMAS

Veterinarian Olivia O'Ballivan finds the animals
in Stone Creek playing Cupid between her and
Tanner Quinn. Even Tanner's daughter, Sophie,
is eager to play matchmaker. With everyone
conspiring against them and the holiday season
fast approaching, Tanner and Olivia may just get
everything they want for Christmas after all!

*Available December 2008
wherever books are sold.*

HARLEQUIN® *Romance*®

Marry-Me Christmas

by *USA TODAY* bestselling author
SHIRLEY JUMP

A *Bride* FOR ALL *Seasons*

Ruthless and successful journalist Flynn never mixes business with pleasure. But when he's sent to write a scathing review of Samantha's bakery, her beauty and innocence catches him off guard. Has this small-town girl unlocked the city slicker's heart?

Available December 2008.

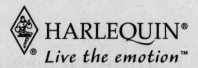

HARLEQUIN®
Live the emotion™

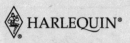

HARLEQUIN®

❯American★Romance®

HOLLY JACOBS
Once Upon a Christmas

Daniel McLean is thrilled to learn he
may be the father of Michelle Hamilton's
nephew. When Daniel starts to spend
time with Brandon and help her organize
Erie Elementary's big Christmas Fair, the
three discover a paternity test won't make
them a family, but the love they discover
just might....

**Available December 2008
wherever books are sold.**

LOVE, HOME & HAPPINESS

www.eHarlequin.com   HAR75242

REQUEST YOUR FREE BOOKS!
2 FREE NOVELS PLUS 2
FREE GIFTS!

HARLEQUIN ROMANCE®

From the Heart, For the Heart

YES! Please send me 2 FREE Harlequin Romance® novels and my 2 FREE gifts (gifts are worth about $10). After receiving them, if I don't wish to receive any more books, I can return the shipping statement marked "cancel". If I don't cancel, I will receive 4 brand-new novels every month and be billed just $3.32 per book in the U.S. or $3.80 per book in Canada, plus 25¢ shipping and handling per book and applicable taxes, if any*. That's a savings of over 15% off the cover price! I understand that accepting the 2 free books and gifts places me under no obligation to buy anything. I can always return a shipment and cancel at any time. Even if I never buy another book, the two free books and gifts are mine to keep forever.

114 HDN ERQW 314 HDN ERQ9

Name _____ (PLEASE PRINT)

Address _____ Apt. #

City _____ State/Prov. _____ Zip/Postal Code

Signature (if under 18, a parent or guardian must sign)

Mail to the **Harlequin Reader Service:**
IN U.S.A.: P.O. Box 1867, Buffalo, NY 14240-1867
IN CANADA: P.O. Box 609, Fort Erie, Ontario L2A 5X3

Not valid to current subscribers of Harlequin Romance books.

Want to try two free books from another line?
Call 1-800-873-8635 or visit www.morefreebooks.com.

* Terms and prices subject to change without notice. N.Y. residents add applicable sales tax. Canadian residents will be charged applicable provincial taxes and GST. Offer not valid in Quebec. This offer is limited to one order per household. All orders subject to approval. Credit or debit balances in a customer's account(s) may be offset by any other outstanding balance owed by or to the customer. Please allow 4 to 6 weeks for delivery. Offer available while quantities last.

Your Privacy: Harlequin Books is committed to protecting your privacy. Our Privacy Policy is available online at www.eHarlequin.com or upon request from the Reader Service. From time to time we make our lists of customers available to reputable third parties who may have a product or service of interest to you. If you would prefer we not share your name and address, please check here. ☐

HR08R

Coming Next Month

Season's greetings from Harlequin Romance®! Festive miracles, mistletoe kisses and winter weddings to get you into the holiday spirit as we bring you Christmas treats aplenty this month....

#4063 CINDERELLA AND THE COWBOY Judy Christenberry

With her two young children in tow, struggling widow Elizabeth stepped onto the Ransom Homestead looking for the family she'd never had. Despite being welcomed with open arms by the children's grandfather, it's blue-eyed rancher Jack who Elizabeth dreams will make their family complete....

#4064 THE ITALIAN'S MIRACLE FAMILY Lucy Gordon
Heart to Heart

Betrayed by their cheating partners, Alysa and Drago strike an unlikely friendship. But Alysa's calm facade hides a painful secret, which twists every time she sees Drago's child. Can the healing miracle of love make them a family?

#4065 HIS MISTLETOE BRIDE Cara Colter

Police officer Brody hates Christmas. Then vivacious Lila arrives in Snow Mountain and tilts his world sideways. But there's a glimmer of sadness in her soulful eyes. Until, snowbound in a log cabin, Brody claims a kiss under the mistletoe....

#4066 HER BABY'S FIRST CHRISTMAS Susan Meier

When millionaire Jared rescues Elise and her cute baby, Molly, and drives them home for the holidays, he finds himself reluctantly drawn to the tiny family. Elise secretly hopes that gorgeous Jared will stay for Molly's first Christmas—and forever!

#4067 MARRY-ME CHRISTMAS Shirley Jump
A Bride for All Seasons

A ruthless and successful journalist, Flynn never mixes business with pleasure. But when he's sent to write a scathing review of Samantha's bakery, her beauty and innocence catches him off guard. Has this small-town girl unlocked the city-slicker's heart?

#4068 PREGNANT: FATHER WANTED Claire Baxter
Baby on Board

There is more to Italian playboy Ric than he lets the world see. And pregnant travel writer Lyssa is determined to find out what. She's fiercely independent, but could Ric, in fact, be the perfect husband and father for her baby?

HRCNM1108